Jazz - alias Jason Smith

For my family...
my inspiration, my universe.

Prologue

Hot sun bakes pale yellow sand.

Overhead the sky, a mixture of light and rich dark purples is scattered with fat, wispy white clouds.

A large oasis fed by an underground spring reflects the purple sky.

Large black rocks edge, tall leafy palms.

A strange sight. An oasis surrounded by sand dunes as far as the eye can see.

Few know of its existence except for the lizards and birds who survive in this place – and the dragons. The dragons rely on its existence.

'Tap, tap, tap ... crack.'

If you weren't listening, you might have missed it.

Sharpspike tilts his head, hops over for a better view of the eggs half-buried in the hot sand. He takes flight.

The tapping continues, is joined by more tapping, until the sound is so loud, you couldn't not hear it.

A small blue head breaks free of a large white egg, followed by a bigger blue-black one, from the same egg. The darker head swings in an arc biting at the smaller blue. The young blue's eyes open wide. Swinging his neck, moving his head out of the way.

'Who are you?'

The blue-black stops. 'Zion.'

'I'm Sian. Don't eat me, brother.'

A moment, a look of realisation. 'Of course not, my brother. Happy hatching day.'

Stretching, they each push with scaly limbs to remove the last of the egg encasing them. Around them many more eggs hatch dragons. One fuchsia takes flight on wobbly wings, landing not far from her egg. Perching on a large black rock, she stretches wings to dry. Red veins trace through translucent pink wings.

She throws back her head ... 'Growl.'

Others look towards the pink and in turn throw back their heads and growl.
The blue-black and blue join in … 'Roar.'

All turn to the two, bobbing heads in acknowledgement – the leaders. All feel it.

'Roar.' The twins take flight on wobbly wings to nearby rocks. Extending wings to the sun. Faces upturned.

Spread across black rocks, all colours and sizes of dragons. Small dragons – some so tiny, the size of a coconut from nose to tip – to the big blue-black who is twice the size of the next largest.

Emerging from the hot sands around the oasis. Made moist by the spring. The perfect hatching ground.

A once in 100-year event – sometimes longer.

Dragons choose carefully when to have their young, so as not to overburden their beautiful world.

Barely 50 dragons. Some eggs remain but those may never hatch. Ants and lizards wait to claim them. No-one watches them. The Z-dragon, Sharpspike, gone. His job, to keep the eggs safe while they incubate, finished.

All focus is on drying wings before finding food. Wings extended to the sun, twisting back and forth to dry each side.

They have a long journey home ahead.

Zion and Sian perch side by side on a black rock. Wings outstretched, snouts face up to the sun. Sian has awoken with the thoughts and memories of his kind. Sharing them now with his brother as they sun themselves. It's why the others recognised them as leaders, they roared, they knew how. Born with the memories made them special. Sian and his brother, Zion, would lead the others home when it was time – they knew the way. The others would soon be able to communicate without speaking. But, as newly hatched, the instinct to feed and grow clouded everything.

Sian felt it first. Something had come. It felt heavy, dark – he wasn't scared but he could feel the weight of it – black and ominous. He shared thoughts with Zion who cocked his head to one side to listen. They squinted into the distance but there was nothing to see but sand. Sian focused on a distant dune and reappeared at the place where he had looked. He searched again. They were there. He shared his vision with Zion.

'Come back, brother. We must hide the others.'

Zion swung his head around seeking a place to hide. They both reached for their father but were not yet strong enough to make contact. Dust appeared over the dune – riders approaching. They shared their vision with the others but they did not respond, unmoved by the image. Sian allowed the dark, oppressive feelings he was experiencing to wash over them.

'Sqwee?' inquired a young female.

'We must hide,' responded Sian in her mind. He shared thoughts with the others. 'You must be quiet, very quiet, and you must not move.'

'Move behind the rocks, now,' Zion thought. 'When we tell you to wrap yourself around the rock as if you are the rock, do so. We will hide you.'

Sian and Zion wrapped themselves across the top of the rock, watching the riders. When they were close, the dragons vanished. The rocks grew around them, enfolding them.

Riders wearing long black robes pulled up their steeds. Dismounting swiftly, they walked to the hatching ground.

Sian threw a thought to Zion. 'The eggs!'

Sian and Zion had not hidden the unhatched eggs.

Bending, a robed figure swung a device over each of the eggs. He selected five of varying sizes. Each was placed in an individual sack. One rider looked briefly at the rocks around the oasis – so black against the bright sand dunes.

All remounted and rode back the way they had come.

Contents

Chapter 1 – Earth

Verillon appeared above the circle of dragons, men and women, leaning on boulders, or sitting on the dirt around a large fire.

A massive dragon – black with scales that shimmered an inky blue. Red flecks from the fire currently danced over his belly scales.

Long hard black talons dug deep into the earth as he landed. Wings stirred clouds of dust and dirt, forcing dragon kin to extend wings to protect the humans. White fangs hung long from a large broad jaw. The black ridge down his spine was bigger than those of any other dragon around the fire. He was the oldest – clear to all present by the size of his ridge.

Speaking for the benefit of the humans, in a deep male voice, he growled, 'I apologise for my tardiness, but I have grave news. The Inkaba have identified a new home. Two planet-sized ships left Sarth today. I saw them from a distance.' Looking up to the sky, he continued, 'I failed to destroy them. They disappeared as I came close.' Pausing, he gazed at each one in the circle. Eyes first, followed by head. 'I fear they are on their way to a new land. We must find these ships and destroy them before they reach their destination. I do not need to remind you of the horror they will bestow on any planet they encounter.' Nods and murmurs of agreement from those around the campfire.

A large red dragon with black tips on every scale spoke. 'Dragon brothers and sisters, it is time. We must leave our beloved Draco. It seems we have once again entered times of war.' Fire skipped across her hide as if some mystical glyph animated her scales. It was not just a reflection. Magic played a part in this display. Large yellow eyes streaked with green watched the group. Half the size of Verillon, she was much younger but still commanded everyone's attention.

Representatives from the Council of the Keepers stood. Some touched heads, others shook hands, grasping elbows at the same time. Each touched the dragons on the right shoulder before departing. Some teleported away, others headed to waiting ships.

All had much to achieve now the Inkaba were on the move.

***

Metal scraped softly against metal. An audible click, then another, and he was free to lift his legs from the lock that held them secure during the flight. He wiggled each leg one at a time and felt the blood begin to flow back through them.

Shifting his torso, he felt stiff, cramped. He hated travelling like this but his father had insisted. The M1 transporter was a discreet ship – easily concealable.

'Stairs.' The leg locks moved again, simulating stairs to ward off blood clots. 'Stop,' he ordered.

'Sigh.'

'Master?'

'It's still the same view out the window, Iz. It hasn't changed in hours, days for that matter. All I can see is blackness dotted with pinpricks of light and swirls of milky whiteness. How much longer before I can really stretch?'

'Five hours before landing,' came a sympathetic female voice.

He'd spent day one studying and listening to beats. Twenty-four hours later and he'd had enough reading and music. Now he was just staring out the window.

The M1 transporter capsule was not built for long voyages – designed for speed and efficiency, not comfort. Bigger, more comfortable ships consume larger amounts of energy and are more suitable for crews, not individual trips. They are also easier to detect. Transporter capsules resembled a large silver bullet with one rounded end. Overall, they maintained a low profile. Big enough to house one full-grown adult with a little room for moving and stretching of limbs but definitely no walking around. M1s have only one window directly opposite their occupant.

Faroon had chosen the capsule for his son, Jazz, himself. Jazz was travelling to his grandparents on Earth and the craft needed to be nondescript and easy to hide once he arrived. Earthlings weren't too comfortable with – make that, aware of – visitors from other planets. Plus, he may just need it for a quick escape.

Jazz is a Pedite. Pedites are a very smart race similar to humans in looks, except for their hair and unusual height. They hail from Micoron, two galaxies from Earth.

Jazz's father is a third-rank Armun – third in command of the planet of Micoron. Armuns were elected to govern the planet on a monthly basis with every resident able to cast their vote electronically via their AI. It was customary for these dignitaries' children to make solo journeys to other planets to learn of other worlds and expand on their substantial education. One day Jazz too could rise to the ranks of Armun, maybe even to the rank of 1st Armun. Jazz's great-grandfather had held the rank of 1st Armun from an early age – the youngest in the history of Micoron.

A dangerous time to be travelling far from home. The Inkaba had almost depleted the resources on Sarth and were looking for a new world to conquer. Their pale blue translucent skin was paired with cone-shaped heads and razor-sharp teeth – the unique features of their race. Their arms and legs are of similar proportions to that of humans and Pedites, albeit extremely muscular by comparison. The similarities to humans and Pedites end there.

Inkaba did little to care for the worlds they inhabited. Once the resources of the planet they populated were gone, the Inkaba moved on. They were warriors who fought well in battle and lived off their plunder. They knew almost nothing about growing crops or refining fuels after they conquered a world. They would force the inhabitants into slavery to complete these tasks for them. For this reason, Jazz's mother, Alala, had fought hard to keep her son at home, even though twelve was an appropriate age to be apprenticed. Alala, afraid for her only son, was barely talking to Faroon when Jazz had left two days earlier.

The capsule was currently piloted by an artificial intelligence system.

The female voice spoke again. 'Master Jazz, are you ready for food?'

'Hey, Iz, not really hungry.'

'We will be entering Earth's atmosphere shortly. Even if the master is not hungry, it would be best to eat now as once we are closer we may experience turbulence.'

'Maybe some "beanz" then, Izzy.'

Isabel and Jazz had been together for six years. Usually she rode with Jazz on a ring he wore but now she piloted the ship having downloaded into it before their departure. She controlled all aspects of the voyage, right down to the temperature of the craft and catering.

'Thanks, Iz,' Jazz said as a small door opened in the wall to his left. A tray, held by a metal arm, emerged. Staring out the window, Jazz chewed each chip thoroughly.

The bluish-green edge of Earth was visible now.

Due to what Jazz considered a design flaw, he could only see out the window in front of him, while his feet pointed towards his destination. Flying in an M1 always felt like hurtling towards nothing. Landing docks for M1s were only a few feet wide and, on approach, the occupant couldn't see the dock at all so had to take a leap of faith that they were on track for landing.

'Iz, log a job with the engineers. They need to add cameras to the top and tail of this craft so occupants can see their approach. Flying so long in this thing with only one window is so tedious. I'm surprised it hasn't been logged already.'

'Message logged, Master. We are entering Earth's atmosphere. Please stow all food in the compartment above and secure all body locks.'

The ship shook. Isabel took a minute to steady the craft.

'You have a face call, Master.'

'Jazz, we just saw you enter the atmosphere on our screen. How was your flight? Josh and Stan are instructing Izzy where to land now. We should see you shortly.'

Zoshwan, known as Josh, was Jazz's grandfather and Frieda, the voice and face beaming on the monitor, was his gran. Both had taken on human names when they decided to live on Earth fifteen years ago.

'Just fine, Gran. How's Porus?'

9

Porus, his grandparents' cat, had unknowingly been brought with them when they last visited Micoron. He'd stowed away in a storage area of their vessel and was located only moments before landing. Porus had caused all kinds of problems with disease control and both Faroon and Josh had been furious with the ship's crew for not detecting the pet onboard. But Porus had become a hit on Micoron. While he was in quarantine, hundreds of people had come to stare at the cat through the glass and thousands had tuned in to watch the live feed, often for hours at a time. Cats were never imported to Micoron – too much of a hazard. So, a cat on the planet had piqued the interest of many.

'Porus is just fine, Jazz. Getting a bit old now. He just lies around a lot, but he'll be happy to see you. Oh, here's your grandfather.'

'Jazz,' boomed a voice over the speakers.

'Y…yes, sir?' Jazz stammered.

'Had a good flight?'

'Yes, sir,' he tried more confidently.

'That's good. I'll see you shortly.' With that the screen winked out.

Jazz's grandfather was a brusque man. Not unkind but his manner was very matter of fact. Even when Jazz had skinned his knee at the age of three, his grandfather had shown little sympathy. As a result, Jazz was a tad intimidated by him, to say the least. On his grandparents' last visit, when he was ten, Jazz had been playing Battlebowl, a game that involved a round ball and a two-ended bat called a punt. The idea was to punt the ball between various goalposts around an oval and score goals. Jazz had, instead, been hit in the mouth by an opposing player's punt. His lip had split and started to bleed. When his mouth began to throb, Jazz looked up to where his grandfather was watching him from the spectator stands. Josh had looked sternly at Jazz until he controlled his urge to cry. Jazz had spent the rest of their visit avoiding his grandfather. Frieda had cried when it was time to return home. She wanted to take Jazz back to Earth for a holiday, complaining through sobs that she had hardly seen her grandson.

The pod moved to an upright position so Jazz was standing. A slight jolt and they were down. The front of the capsule popped open and Jazz was met by a smiling face. The sun was almost gone, so Frieda carried a torch which she shone on Jazz's face.

'My goodness, you've grown tall. How was your flight? Come, your grandfather's at the house.'

Shielding his eyes, Jazz turned to the ship. 'Iz, are you going to be right to hide the cap?' He scoured the landscape. 'Over there looks like a great spot, among those trees. Can you sense them?'

'Yes, Master. I've detected them on the ship's systems.'

Turning to walk with his Gran, Jazz continued, 'Oh, and Izzy, don't forget to switch back to mobile.' He needn't have mentioned it but knowing Izzy was with him eased his nerves.

'I am here,' she spoke from the ring on his finger.

He hadn't seen an Earth dwelling before. Jazz's eyes grew wide as they walked towards a large square brick building. It was surrounded by shaded platforms on which stood chairs and tables made of wood.

'Strange that they should make furniture from wood, Iz,' he whispered.

'Woof, woof.'

A four-legged, brown furry creature with a white stripe down the centre of its forehead bounded toward them. Jumping in front of Frieda, Jazz dropped into a half crouch, raised his right hand and yelled, 'Stun, straight ahead!'

Zing!

A green light shot from his ring.

'Jazz, no!' Too late. The green light hit the creature. With a yelp it froze in mid-air, before falling on its side.

'Oh, Jazz, that was Sam.'

Jazz, momentarily pleased with himself, turned to his gran.

'Sam ... what's a Sam?'

'Sam is a dog. He's friendly. He was just coming to say hello.'

Frieda hurried towards Sam. Jazz followed, rather confused now. He was not sure about this dog thing so stayed a couple of steps behind his gran. When Frieda reached Sam, she knelt, placing her hand on his black chest.

'It's okay. He's still breathing. How long is your stun set for?'

'Just a few minutes,' Jazz said, raising an eyebrow.

'Good. We'll just leave him here then. No doubt he will wake up shortly.'

Standing, she continued towards the house. Jazz followed, still curious about the Sam but, realising that, given the pace Frieda was setting, she would be inside the house before him and he might have to encounter his grandfather alone.

Chapter 2 – Foe

Thirty years ago, the Inkaba had arrived on Sarth, a small planet with a surface area similar to that of the country he had just landed in, Australia – seven and a half million square kilometres, give or take. There was little chance for the Sarthians to defend their world against the invader's overwhelming force. Luckily, the Sarthians had a well-equipped flying fleet and, in the six months it took the Inkaba to conquer the entire planet, it had been possible to evacuate the inhabitants of Sarth to nearby planets, including many to Micoron.

Following the invasion of Sarth, the Council of Keepers had come together to construct a battle plan to defeat the Inkaba and take back the planet for its Keepers. Unfortunately for the Sarthians, the Council arrived at an alternate decision. Instead of an invasion, they would leave the Inkaba on Sarth till they moved on again. This plan was devised to minimise fatalities that would certainly ensue from engaging the Inkaba in battle. Most planets preferred peace and, after all, the Sarthians were safe for now. Leaving the Inkaba undisturbed also reduced the threat to the military forces of neighbouring planets.

The Council of Keepers was comprised of representatives from all the known friendly planets and universes. Their job: to keep the peace between the planets by ensuring all followed the universal Keepers Law. The rules were simple:

Keepers Law States:
   One must not inhabit another's planet without authorisation.
   One must not undertake projects that affect Universe rotations and equilibrium.
   One must not kill outside one's home planet.

The rules made certain that what happened on each planet did not affect other planets or universes.

***

Captain Trane of the Inkaba stood behind an imposing silver table in the control tower of Picton, the former capital of Sarth. The room was large with white walls but contained only the oval table surrounded by a hundred white stools. Most were occupied but Trane was awaiting the arrival of the remainder of Inkaba's invasion captains before speaking.

As the final commanders took their seats, Trane looked up, noting the late arrivals – his loathing of dawdlers well known. 'Later,' he muttered under his breath. The latecomers knew backlash was imminent and kept their eyes lowered for fear of further retribution. No excuse would be of use.

'Our scouts have returned,' growled Trane. 'Preliminary observations identify a red centre as the ideal landing site for our fleets. The lands are scarcely inhabited. We could easily set down without drawing attention. Ready your forces. We leave in twenty days. Dismissed.'

All turned to leave. Trane motioned for his assistant Actool to approach.

'Those latecomers, captains Orsel and Waith, ration their troops, and remove their recreation leave. They will not be so casual about attending next time. Go now.'

Chapter 3 – New Day

Following his arrival, after the long flight, Jazz had taken a short tour of his grandparents' house. It was not extensive, containing just four sleeping quarters, two refreshing suites, a large entertainment/eating space and a separate food preparation area.

Jazz's grandfather had not met them on arrival because an important transmission had come through from Micoron. Since Jazz's capsule had entered Earth's atmosphere, his grandfather had been locked in what Frieda called 'the office'. Frieda and Jazz enjoyed some sweet warm milk before sleep started to overcome him and Frieda hustled him into one of the sleeping quarters with the promise they would talk more tomorrow.

Morning came.

Waking, he squinted as sunlight beamed through a crack in the curtains. Reclining on a large bed that was made of wood, he looked around. There was a wooden desk and matching chair in one corner and a round, red, shaggy rug covering the brown tiled floor.

Hum … mm.

A fan cooling the room from above drew his attention.

Thick, muggy air made him tug at his long-sleeved flight suit as sweat trickled down his back, plastering the hair to the back of his neck.

Travel bags sat on the floor beside the bed. Isabel must have organised their arrival while he slept. Functional objects from Micoron like these contained technology that often allowed them to fly or roll with AI direction.

He had taken Earth studies before setting off and it was now time to put that research to good use. Getting up, he pulled the bed straight and opened his suitcase. Alala had packed him some garments made of Earth fabrics. T-shirts and shorts were the same universally, but fabrics were not. His shirt was made from a heavy material and his shorts from something even thicker. Micoron fabrics were light, more akin to silk.

He crossed the hall to the refreshing suite, closed the door, enclosing himself in a completely wood-panelled room. The walls were finished in a light pine, which continued around a white bathtub and a white sink. The dark chocolate tiles under his feet were cool and he felt a moment's relief from the stifling heat.

The shower was large and he adjusted the water temperature to cold. Running his tongue along his teeth he called out to Iz.

'Iz, can you grab my refreshing bag?'

'Morning, Jazz, and no,' Iz dropped formalities as the flight recorder was no longer logging a journey.

'What?' Slightly puzzled, he rinsed soap out of his eyes as if to help him understand.

'I have the same problem I encountered last night, I fear. I can command your refreshing bag to your sleeping quarter's door but I cannot command the door to open to allow passage. Frieda helped last night opening doors for me.' He detected mirth in Isabell's response. 'You may have to go and get it yourself.'

Grinning, he responded, 'Sounds like my education has already commenced then, Iz.'

After showering and dressing, he retrieved his own toiletries.

Frieda sat at a large wooden table next to the food preparation area, reading a large black-and-white paper and drinking what smelt like Koor from a mug.

'Morning, Jazz. Did you sleep well?' she asked, not looking up from her cup.

'Yes, thanks, Gran.'

She smiled, finally looking up. 'Good. Hungry? Isabel, does Jazz have any allergies? I can't quite remember but his father was always allergic to anything made of cows' milk on this planet.'

'No, ma'am,' replied Isabel from Jazz's finger. 'Nothing has ever bothered my master except Wersal fur back home, but that just causes him to sneeze. Not life threatening.'

'Good. Toast, pancakes, eggs, cereal, what will it be then?'

'Hmm ... eggs or pancakes? Can I have eggs and pancakes, Gran? Mum doesn't actually cook much back home and I can't really remember having pancakes cooked by anyone other than Isabel and the cooker.'

The cooker was an oven, fridge, slicer and dicer machine on Micoron that could take your order and prepare it all in one.

'No offence, Iz. Yours are great but they always come out tasting purrrfect. Sometimes it's nice for things to taste like something is missing.'

'None taken, Master. Mistress Frieda, is there somewhere I can patch into the house so I might gain access to door control and general appliances? I can't seem to locate your hub, just the main computer in the office, but he won't talk to me. He's busy transmitting for Master Josh.'

'Just Frieda is fine, Isabel. Unfortunately, the house isn't wired like those back home. We just didn't see the need and the house was already built when we bought it. It would have been too large a job. Josh would have had to do it himself as these Earthlings would question the need for such cabling. Stan, Josh's IA, just travels with him on his finger as you do with Jazz but he can take control of Josh's computer, car and a couple of appliances when asked.'

'Stan,' called Frieda.

'Yes, ma'am,' a deep voice replied from the radio on the kitchen bench.

'Where's Josh, Stan?'

'Sleeping on the couch,' came the reply. 'He didn't finish till five this morning. Micoron did not stop transmitting till well after 1.00 am. Master was then kept busy talking to various members of the Keepers. I believe the matter was quite urgent but I will leave the details to the master to explain further.'

Frowning, Frieda chewed her top lip.

'Gran, is everything okay?'

'Hmm, oh yes. Stan, could you show Isabel the ropes? Let her know what you can and can't do in this house. Also, can you download the schematics of Jacobs High School for Isabel? Jazz will need to start there in three days and it would assist if he knew where he was going. Oh, and don't think I didn't notice that comment about my pancakes and eggs not being perfect, young man. You're lucky I have met the cooker.' Smiling distractedly, she swiped at Jazz with a dish towel and opened the fridge, pulling out eggs, milk, flour and butter. She bustled around the kitchen while Jazz took a seat at the table.

'A new school! Am I excited, Iz? We were popular at our old school but everything here is different. Do you think we'll fit in? What about my hair?' he said, reaching to touch his orange locks.

People of Micoron had one of three hair colours: white blond, jet black or bright orange. Their hair also grew exceptionally fast. Since leaving Micoron two days ago, Jazz's hair had already grown a couple of centimetres.

'And what about my height?' he exclaimed.

Although only twelve in human years, he was already tall. Standing at least 10 centimetres taller than most in his year.

***

'Sigh.'

Faroon sat in his book room behind a large black desk, hands resting together his two pointer fingers forming a peak, the remainder curled into a fist. He was staring absently at the screen above his desk.

Thinking about the report he had just read, he flicked to another screen. Jazz's shuttle showed it would be landing soon, good he was almost safe. He went back to his ruminations, he'd share the news with all Keepers very soon. His assistant coordinating contact now.

The report had advised the Inkaba scout ships were seen returning to Sarth. Five days later, massive transporter ships departed. This could mean only one thing. Without slaves to mine or farm, supplies must be almost exhausted. Resources on Sarth have been depleting for years.

Faroon reflected on what he knew of the Inkaba. They knew nothing of farming, industry or mining. Fighting and pillaging being their forte, with few skills other than war. A lack of slaves meant what is stolen by them was soon depleted.

The upside is that, when they leave, the people of Sarth will be able to return to their planet and slowly, over time, rebuild. It will be challenging but other planets will assist. Sarth has always been abundant in natural resources and many planets had sorely missed what Sarthians used to supply to the Universal trade market. Sarth may even get more help than the usual assistance rendered any planet in trouble but this is not good news for the planet earmarked for the impending Inkaba invasion. If the Council of Keepers can't find information about the Inkaba's plans and warn the target planet, its inhabitants could be forced into slavery and their planet eventually ruined.

Faroon would speak with his father, Josh, shortly. Josh sat high in the Council of Keepers. After all, he was the Keeper of Earth. Earth hadn't made contact with other planets in their universe yet and it was important to the Council of Keepers that they come to this in their own time. For this reason, Josh had been asked to live on the planet and act on its behalf, relaying information back to the Keepers and watching to ensure all was well.

There were a few hundred other Micoronians living on Earth. Most had gone there to retire or get back to nature, away from the fast-paced life of Micoron. Therefore, it was also Josh's job to ensure these inhabitants behaved themselves and did not draw attention to their alien race.

***

'It's important you have a human name and you're probably the best person to choose one,' Freida said as she handed him a book of baby names, a deep frown on her forehead. 'My only advice, pick a name like your own or you might forget to answer if people call you.'

'Thanks for breakfast, Gran,' said Jazz. He grabbed his last pancake, folding it in half to take with him.

On the porch, Jazz once again crossed paths with Sam. Sam sat next to a grey outdoor settee, licking Porus about the ears. Enjoying the bath, Porus noticed Jazz watching and swatted at Sam as he stood to rub himself against Jazz's legs, purring. Sam on the other hand wasn't quite as friendly.

He barked as he jumped off the porch, reseating himself about five metres away with one eye suspiciously trained on Jazz.

Jazz couldn't blame him. There were no ill effects from such a short stun but waking up in a different situation could be confusing. Sam would have remembered running towards people then waking up alone and in the dark. When Jazz was younger, he used the stun setting when he played hide-and-seek with his cousins. This ensured no-one cheated. Of course, the adults forbade it, so it was done completely without their knowledge.

Jazz sat and opened the book to 'J'. Frieda and Josh had already taken Smith as their last name, so Jazz only had to come up with a first name.

'You would assume this would be easy, Iz. But what if I choose badly? Who wants to be called by a name they hate for a year, or worse, what if I chose a lame name and I get laughed at? No, this is a serious task and requires some serious thought,' he announced.

'Hmm ... Jack, John, Jill – oops, not for me – Jerry, Jack, already said that, Jacob, Julian, nope, Jester ... augh, this is going to take me all afternoon.'

After half an hour, he mumbled, 'Hmm ... Jason. That doesn't sound too bad, it means something to do with healer.' Louder this time, he said, 'Jason Smith! Jazz alias Jason Smith. I might just get used to that. Hey, Izzy, what do you think? My name is Jason Smith.'

'Very good. I like it. Should I call you by that name from now on?' replied Izzy.

'Yes, please. Maybe then I will actually get used to answering to it'.

***

Making her way down to the study where Josh was lying on the couch, Frieda opened the door slowly so as not to wake him. The air-conditioner was cooling the room so Frieda grabbed the blanket off the armrest and placed it over her husband. Josh opened his eyes, grabbing one of Frieda's hands affectionately.

'Sorry, I didn't mean to wake you.'

'That's okay, I think I have had enough sleep now.' He sat up, patting the seat next to him.

'So, what's the news from home? Is there something wrong? You were locked in here for hours last night.'

'Not too good, I'm afraid. The Inkaba ships, the ones they call Arcs, have left Sarth. That can mean only one thing: they have found a new planet.'

'Does our son have any idea where they are going?'

'No, not at this stage, but all the Keepers are on high alert and there are large numbers of troops scouring the universe for any signs of Inkaba scouts. How's the boy?'

'Oh, Josh, it's wonderful to have him here and he's grown so much. He's out on the porch choosing his Earth name as we speak. Are you going to go and talk to him soon? I think he knows there is something wrong, too. I'm not sure how much he knows about the potential Inkaba move. His father usually keeps him abreast of all political issues, though, so I think he would want Jazz to know. After all, he will be another set of Alien eyes here on Earth.'

'Yes. Faroon requested I let him know as soon as we spoke. I will go see him now.'

'Master,' came Stan from his ring.

'Yes, Stan?'

'Isabel, Jazz's AI, informs me he has chosen the name Jason for himself and I believe he would like to start using this name immediately.'

'Good. Thanks, Stan. Let Isabel know I'm coming. That boy always seems to be jumpy around me, so I don't want to sneak up on him. Frieda, there isn't much more to Faroon's report other than that they are on the move but if I think of anything I have forgotten, I will tell you a bit later. What time is it? Have I missed breakfast?' Josh asked, pulling down the corners of his mouth at her in an attempt to look pitiful. 'Can you whip me up a little bacon and eggs?'

'Oh, you,' she replied, nudging her husband on the arm, 'go talk to the boy and I will make your breakfast. What I need is a cooker like back home.'

***

Isabel let Jason know Josh was coming. The two of them had been exploring the grounds, checking out their new surroundings. Josh and Frieda lived on a five-acre block. The house was surrounded by grass and big weeping trees with some native bush across the back of the block. Jason knew that they lived on a continent called Australia and their home was in the north of that continent in the Northern Territory. Next to the house on the left there was a large shed which housed various tools and what he guessed was his grandfather's car. It was a large car that Iz had informed him was a LandCruiser. A smaller Pulsar, which must be Frieda's, sat next to it.

On hearing Isabel's news, Jason left the garage and headed back towards the porch. Josh was already sitting on the grey settee with iced drinks, waiting for him.

'How goes it, Jason?' Josh asked.

'Well, thank you, Grandfather, and you?' he said, smiling at the use of his new name.

'Yeah, not bad, not bad, but come sit down. I have a few serious things to discuss with you. I have been speaking to your father. He says your schooling is excellent and that you are good at sports. Is that correct?'

'Yes, sir.'

'I don't want to see that lapse on my watch or there'll be trouble.' The boy flinched ... Damn! He hadn't meant that to come out so rough – he had been aiming for humour.

'Yes, sir.'

'Also, the Inkaba scouts have been spotted returning to Sarth and Arcs left not long after. Keep your eyes peeled, son, we need all the help we can get with these heathens. Do you know what you're looking for?'

'Yes, sir.'

'Good. You should go see if your grandmother has any chores for you.'

Josh finished his drink and went out to the shed via the kitchen where he turned his bacon and eggs into a sandwich that he took with him. Soon after, Jason heard the LandCruiser start up and saw Josh backing out of the driveway.

'Well, Iz, that went okay, don't you think? Chores, though ... huh, what are chores?'

'Small jobs that get things done around the house. Human kids do them for their parents to obtain wages, or pocket money, to spend on things they want. Could be interesting, Jason. You haven't had pocket money before. Micoron transaction cards are all billed back to your father. Money would allow you to purchase whatever you like.'

'Hmm ... could be interesting, Isabel, and I am looking forward to this school thing also, I think. Let's just hope we fit in.'

Chapter 4 – New School

The next couple of days were a flurry of chores, collecting books and uniforms, crash courses from his grandmother regarding Earth etiquette and a mix of breakfasts, lunches and dinners which his grandmother taught him to cook for himself in case they went out. After all, Isabel couldn't cook for him. But that didn't mean that Isabel couldn't recite back the instructions verbatim.

All too soon it was his first day – the day of reckoning. It started well. The weather was muggy again but Jason had taken to wearing just some cotton pyjama bottoms to bed. He was dressed in his uniform, sitting at the breakfast table when his grandfather walked in from outside, a very tall gentleman with bright orange hair behind him. Talking quickly to each other, they hardly noticed Jason sitting at the table, eating. Stan must have said something as Josh glanced down at his hand then looked at the table.

'Morning, Jason,' Josh said, stopping mid-stride. 'This is Walter. Walter is from Micoron. Walter, my grandson Jazz. He has taken the name of Jason while on Earth.'

'Morning, Jason.' Walter turned, laying a beaming smile on Jason. 'Enjoying our lovely weather?' In addition to Walter's height and bright orange hair, he had round rosy cheeks that lit up when he smiled.

'Morning, sirs,' replied Jason. 'It's my first day of school today.'

'Oh,' Walter raised an eyebrow, 'are you looking forward to school then, young Jason?'

'Yes, yes, sir,' colour flushing his cheeks as he tried to recover from his outburst.

Smiling warmly, Walter continued, 'Good for you, Son. An education is gold in this life,' and with that he turned, following Josh down the hall.

'Iz,' said Jason,' chewing his cereal thoughtfully, 'Walter seems nice. I wonder how long he has lived here. And what is gold?'

A few moments passed before Isabel processed his questions. 'Farah says almost five years now. He lives here with a young daughter half your age.' Farah was Walter's intelligence system. If you ever needed to know something about someone you could usually find out by having your intelligence system talk to their intelligence system. Of course, they would only ever divulge information that their masters allowed. 'And gold is a valuable commodity.'

'Jason, what are you doing? You're going to be late. Go get your bag and I will run you down in Josh's car. You can take the bike in the shed from tomorrow.' Freida stopped and looked at Jason thoughtfully. 'Can you ride a bike?'

'Sure,' said Jason. Pausing, he added, 'What's a bike?'

Freida smiled. 'Never mind. I'll show you tonight and we should have you riding within the week. Come on, get a wriggle on. I'll meet you in the car.' There was another long pause before Jason heard Freida yell from outside, 'And don't forget your lunch.'

He ran to the fridge and was still cramming his lunch into his bag as Freida started up the car. He jumped in the front.

'Mr Walker, the principal, is expecting you to visit Reception,' said Freida. 'Do you want me to come?'

'No thanks, Gran. Not sure how it works on this planet but taking your grandmother to school at home would be considered rather lame.'

Laughing softly, she replied, 'Yes, I think it's probably the same here. I'll just drop you near the school and you can make your way to the entrance. It's marked quite well. Mr Walker has been sent copies of your transcripts, obviously doctored to suit an Earth school, along with our story that you have transferred from the States where you lived with your parents who have been travelling a lot lately and wanted you to have a bit more stability. Here we are. Have fun. Would you like me to pick you up this afternoon?'

'Actually, Gran, do you mind if I try walking? I sort of know the way and if I get lost, Iz knows where to go.'

'That's fine. Come straight home, though. Once you're a bit more settled you can dawdle a bit but, just for the meantime, I want to know you have made it home. Don't talk to any strangers on the way home and, Iz, stay alert. There are a few not so nice characters on Earth just as there are on Micoron but they won't be afraid of his father here.'

'Yes, Mrs Smith,' replied Isabel formerly.

Jumping out of the car with a wave, he walked towards the school gates. Behind the gates was a mass of kids all wearing the same blue polo shirts and blue shorts as he had on. Some sat talking, others tossed balls, joking and laughing. Moments later he came upon a sign that indicated the office was to the left.

He entered the office and looked around. Inside, behind a large wraparound counter, sat an older woman with short greying hair. The office smelt familiar – musty, like books – instantly reminding him of his father's book room. Faroon boasted a very large, very rare collection of books, a small number from Micoron, the rest ancient volumes from various planets, including Earth. Housed among his most prized possessions were old hieroglyphics on papyrus scrolls his dad had bought from some Egyptian folk that had moved to Zar years before. As it happened, Earth hadn't always been ignorant of Alien species and had only lost that knowledge in the last thousand years or so. The alien race that once settled on the planet Earth were nomads and had eventually chosen to continue their travels across the cosmos.

As he neared the desk, the woman looked up. She was wearing blue-framed glasses and rather garish red lipstick. When she smiled, he noticed the lipstick also covered some teeth.

As he heard *brriiinngg*, he ducked rather quickly behind the desk.

Isabel spoke to him through a small earpiece implanted in his ear. 'That's the school bell. It tells students when their classes are starting. You will hear it a few times during the day for breaks between lessons and end of day.'

'Yes, son, can I help you?' the woman asked, peering over the desk.

Sheepishly, Jason stood. 'My name is Jason, Jason Smith. It's my first day.'

'Just a minute,' she replied. Jason read her name, Edna, off a rather faded gold badge pinned to the front of her blue sweater. She got up from the desk and went to a filing cabinet against the wall. Taking this opportunity to look around, he noted pale yellow walls with a honey-coloured wood trim. Two boys, looking rather morose, sat on a wooden bench along the far wall.

A tall, thin lady with salt and pepper hair opened a door in the wall opposite the bench and looked down her nose at the two boys.

'Bradley and Jamie, follow me please. Mr Walker will see you now.'

Both boys got up and followed her through the door.

Turning, Edna waved a piece of paper at him. 'Here it is, son. Here are your classes and a map to show you where you're going. Your first period is with Ms Martin. Homeroom has just commenced. You just have to cross the quad to reach it – room number 11. Now hurry up, don't dawdle, homeroom only goes for twenty minutes and then you will be off to your next class, which is listed on this piece of paper. Refer to the map so you know where you're going and you should be fine.'

'Yes, ma'am,' replied Jason.

Just then, a girl entered the office. She had dark brown, curly hair with great big blue eyes and a scattering of freckles across her nose. 'This is for you, Edna. Mrs Laroo asked me to bring it over.'

'Thanks, Sally. Oh, Sally, this is Jason. He's just started. Can you show him to Ms Martin's classroom? He's in room 11, right next to Mrs Laroo.'

'Sure, Edna.'

Turning to Jason, her gaze hit his chest and travelled up to his face. As she noticed his bright orange hair, her eyes grew wide. Recovering her composure, she extended her right hand. 'Hi. I'm Sally.'

Isabel spoke in Jason's ear. 'Shake her hand. It's a greeting.'

Jason remembered seeing it in some of his research but unfortunately stuck out his left hand and ended up grabbing her on the back of her right hand and shaking it.

'Close,' said Isabel with mildly sarcastic humour, once again presenting as more human than android. 'Next time use the other hand.'

Jason could feel the heat rising in his face again. Trying to distract her from his bright red face he announced, 'I'm Jason. I'm new.'

Not sure he could go any redder, he smiled, trying to recover his composure.

Sally returned his smile. 'Come along then,' she said brightly. 'Better not keep Ms Martin waiting, or Mrs Laroo, for that matter.'

Crossing a large grassed area, Sally explained it was called The Quad and was where students could sit and eat their lunch or play music. There were also a number of other spots to sit depending on where and who you decided to hang out with. The school, he noted as they walked, was two storeys and made of old, red, dusty bricks.

'There you are,' she said pointing in the direction of Jason's classroom as she entered the adjacent room.

Jason reached for the handle of the blue door, noting the number 11 painted on it, and took a deep breath. As he opened the door and stepped inside, everyone in the room turned to the newcomer and Jason once again glowed red.

It was second semester so most of the other students had already spent half a year together. Towering over all of them, with his bright orange hair, he was the new boy in Ms Martin's Year 8 homeroom and hence the most interesting person in the room. Certainly, if the looks he was receiving were anything to go by.

'Welcome,' said a tall, dark-haired lady, wearing a high-collared blue shirt and dark blue knee-length skirt. 'You must be Jason. We have just taken the roll and I noticed a new name, Jason Smith. You can take a seat over there next to Brett.'

Looking at where she was pointing, he saw one of the boys who had been sitting in the office. Jason wondered how he had got there so quickly.

'Thanks,' replied Jason. He took his seat, shooting a puzzled look at Brett.

'I see you have met Brad,' whispered Brett under his breath. 'He's my brother – my twin brother. No doubt you came from the office, where he lives. He's always in trouble. He and Jamie thought it would be funny to egg Principal Walker's car over the holidays. Great plan, except they did it while he was parked at the shops getting funds from the ATM and the bank's security cameras took photos of them. They'll be on detention for sure and the day's hardly begun. Mum's going to be wild. Was she in the office too?'

'Not that I saw,' whispered Jason.

Brett jumped.

'Are you alright?' asked Jason.

'Yes, it's my mobile. It's set on vibrate.' Slipping it out of his pocket under the desk to read. 'It's Mum. She must want to know what Brad is in trouble for before she gets here.' He replied, mumbling the words under his breath: '*Brad egged walker's car holidays, got caught*' and finished with a frowning emoji.

'How do you know that Walker found out it was your brother?'

'Sally told me – she's Walker's daughter.'

'Brett, do you want to join your brother?' asked the teacher in a stern voice. Snickers broke out across the classroom.

'No, Ms Martin,' he replied, blushing.

'Good. Now what was I saying? Oh yes ... it's important that everyone understands that the school camp this year will be held in Alice Springs and, although it's not until the end of September, we need to start fundraising now so that everybody is able to attend. Therefore, if any of you have any great ideas about how we can raise money, then please share and we will consider them.'

Brriiinngg

'That's the bell. What have you got now?' Brett asked.

'I have no idea.' Pulling his schedule from his pocket, Jason scanned it quickly. 'Looks like Maths with a Mr Perdy.'

'You're with me and Sally then,' confirmed Brett, standing up. 'Come along. Perdy doesn't really like dawdlers and you don't want to be on his radar first day of school. I already live on his radar because most people can't tell Brad and me apart. Everybody except Walker that is, and probably only because Brad spends so much time in his office.'

Outside, they joined Sally.

'Sally, this is Jason. He's new.'

'We've met.'

'Met?' Brett raised an eyebrow. 'How could you have met? It's his first day, he just got here.'

'Ahh, but don't forget I know everyone and everything,' Sally replied with a wink.

Brett scowled. 'Cheesy, very cheesy. Oh no, now I am going to be late for sure.'

Jason and Sally followed Brett's gaze. Walking across the quad was a petite woman wearing blue jeans and a white T-shirt. Blonde hair hung loose above her shoulders as she towed two identical young girls, both with dark brown hair and brown eyes.

'Brett's mum. She basically lives here,' muttered Sally under her breath. 'Hi, Mrs Ranwick,' she said louder as she waved.

'Morning, Sally. Is your dad in a good mood this morning?'

'He's fine, Mrs Ranwick, and the eggs didn't ruin the paint. The boys will probably get two weeks this time, though. He warned them after they took our letterbox.'

'Brett, did you know anything about the eggs?' she turned to Brett.

'Yes,' he said looking at his shoes.

'Well, couldn't you have warned me I'd have to come down today? Your sisters are supposed to start their first day of kindy today and now they are late.'

'Sorry, Mum. Sally only told me this morning that Brad actually got caught. She's been visiting her aunt in Melbourne so I didn't get the inside scoop till today.'

Sighing, Mrs Ranwick said, 'Oh okay, thanks Sally. You kids better get off to class then. I'll go see your dad.'

The three walked off a short distance before Sally commented, 'Your poor mum. Could you imagine having two sets of twins, Jason?'

'Least she didn't twig I had known about the egging for weeks.'

'You knew about it for weeks?' Sally stopped, turning to face Brett. 'And you didn't tell me? You know I wouldn't have said anything.'

'Sally,' replied Brett, 'what did you do all holidays?'

'Oh,' she replied sheepishly. 'Of course.' Pausing, she continued, 'You could have texted.'

Rolling his eyes, Brett said, 'Come on, we're all definitely late now. *Beep beep beep*. Jason, you're definitely on Perdy's radar now too.'

The rest of the day went so quickly Jason barely had time to take it in. Of the six classes he was enrolled in, either Sally or Brett were in four. Brett's twin,

Brad, joined them in science but sat with his mate from the office, laughing and joking at the back of the room.

As the last school bell rang, Jason was scribbling his English homework down off the blackboard.

'The book you need to read this term is *Great Expectations* by Charles Dickens,' their English teacher had informed them. 'You have two months to read the whole book but after each chapter you'll form groups to present a verbal report to the class.'

During English, Sally had sat with a friend near the back of the class, passing notes with some girls nearby. A couple of the girls walked past looking at Jason before they caught his eye, giggling, then left hurriedly through the door. As Sally came up behind him, Jason looked confused.

'What was that for?' He nodded towards the door, a slight scowl on his face, absently touching his orange hair.

'Oh, they have decided you look like someone famous – Rupert Grint from the Harry Potter films. I told them you were from America and now they want to know if you're related. Are you?'

'Am I what?'

'Related to Rupert Grint?'

'I've never heard of him,' said Jason, 'so I shouldn't think so.'

'Shame,' said Sally. 'Would have been cool to have someone semi-famous at school. Oh well, come on then.'

They caught up with Brett and Brad outside.

'Where do you live?' asked Brett.

'Number 17 Oak,' replied Jason.

'Cool. We'll walk with you. We're off one of the streets that runs off Oak, Grevillia. Oh, by the way, this is Brad,' said Brett.

'Howdy,' said Brad. 'I saw you in the office this morning. You in trouble or new?'

'New,' replied Jason.

'Pity,' replied Brad. 'Would have been nice for someone to take the heat off Jamie and me.'

31

'You know,' said Brett sarcastically, 'you could just stay out of trouble. That would take the heat off you.'

Smiling, Brad punched his brother on the arm. Brett winced, rubbing his biceps.

The boys headed off.

'Sally would usually walk with us,' said Brett. 'Her dad mustn't be busy first day back as they are going out to dinner.'

The boys turned off down Grevillia and Jason was finally able to speak freely with Isabel.

'So, Isabel, how did you find school?'

'That should have been my question. Very busy and very noisy, lots of chatter. I don't know how you were able to concentrate. Did you get all your homework? I feel useless not being able to read your homework notes off the boards. It's bad enough I can hardly see anything,' she sulked.

On Micoron she'd see everything by patching into cameras, school equipment, video screens and CCTV. Now, riding on Jason's finger, she was mostly blind except for a small camera on the front of it that looked like a black gem.

'It's okay, Isabel. There wasn't that much. Most of it was setting homework plans and expectations not actual work straightaway. Besides, it's fun. I feel very self-sufficient.'

Chapter 5 – The Meeting

Reaching the gate, he started down the long dirt driveway. Halfway along, he heard a commotion and broke into a run. As he neared the house, Jason found his grandmother yelling at a glass on the table. To his amazement, the glass moved about half a metre up in the air, then down to the table again.

'Gran?'

'Oh, you're home,' said Frieda. 'Whistle, appear!' she yelled.

'What?' replied the glass.

'Appear!' yelled Frieda louder.

A small scaly hand emerged, followed by an arm, a torso, some wings and a large scaly head with big dark brown eyes and spikes on the crown.

A Z-dragon, one of the smaller species of dragons from Draco, a planet of dragons. Brown scales shimmered green when he moved. Talons extended from web-like hands and two fangs, roughly seven centimetres long, jutted from his smiling mouth. Fully visible, he was sitting at the table, his stumpy tail hanging out the back of the chair.

'Hello, Jazz. I'm Whistle. Met you years ago when you were but a hatchling.'

'Oh, hello,' Jason replied bemused.

'What?' replied Whistle.

'Turn up your earpiece,' yelled Frieda.

'What?' asked Whistle, cocking his head to one side.

Frieda tapped on her ear with her index finger then pointed up. Whistle nodded then started fiddling with his ear.

'Can you hear me now?'

'Yes, yes. Very well,' replied Whistle.

'Thank goodness,' said Frieda. 'Now, what are you doing so far from your planet? I didn't want to yell that out before in case the neighbours heard me. They're a fair way away but they might hear. You obviously don't hear as well as you used to.'

Whistle gave a hearty laugh. 'Well, see how you're doing when you celebrate your 300th birthday. All this listening is overrated.'

'Now, Jason, how you enjoying Earth?'

'Well, thank you, sir.'

'Good, one of my favourite planets. Mind you, have to remain invisible all the time. Gives me a bit of a complex – people always looking through me. Not used to dragons, Earthlings you see. Think they would get a fright if they saw me flying overhead.' He laughed, a little flame and smoke escaping from his nostrils.

'So, you're just visiting then?' asked Jason, smiling at the dragon's sense of humour.

'No, no, boy. I wish. No, have been asked to come. Watch the planet to ensure that no Inkaba have set up camp anywhere in the realm. After all, the Earthlings don't know to look for themselves.'

'Wow, there's a lot of land to cover. That will take you forever,' said Jason.

'I not alone. There are many Z-dragons arriving on this planet as we speak. All of us will do a preliminary sweep. Then some will leave. The remainder stay and keep a vigil. Your planet is not under great threat. It is much bigger than usual planets Inkaba try and inhabit. But again, Earthlings know nothing of this threat so we must protect them. And that, my Frieda, is the answer to your question also.'

'Oh, good,' replied Frieda. 'You didn't bring your brother Zip did you? You know what trouble he got into last time, swimming around in that lake uncloaked. Took years for that rumour to subside. Some sort of monster in a lake. Josh won't be very amused if Zip is here.'

Whistle laughed, a deep, throaty, almost-growl laugh with no fire and only a little puff of smoke this time.

'No, Frieda, he's not been back for many a year. Received a very stern warning from the Council of Keepers after that episode. Don't think he cares much for Earth anymore. He's gone to sweep a few other planets with dragon leaders. He hasn't managed to get them offside yet. Even after all these years. Some of my other siblings and kin are here though.'

Dragon leaders were full-sized dragons that lived on the planet Draco. Massive creatures that grew many metres in length and continued to grow in size throughout their entire life. The most powerful creatures in the known universes, both mystical and magical. They rarely came to Earth. Cloaking themselves caused considerable energy disruption, affecting bird migrations and bats' echolocation. Only an emergency would make them take such action. The Council of Keepers would often attend Draco to meet with the dragon leaders. The leaders loved their planet with its beautiful forests and purple skies, two moons and red sun, and they rarely left it. Most races accepted that and, out of respect for these elders, hundreds of years old, went to visit instead of the other way around. The planet was so beautiful no-one minded. For dragon leaders to be performing sweeps of planets other than their own, indicated the urgency of the Keepers' quest.

'So, Whistle,' asked Jason, 'can you perform magic too?'

'Of course,' replied Whistle. 'All dragons are magical.'

With that he disappeared and re-appeared at the other end of the table.

'That of course is also how I got here from my planet. I can look at something and then appear there or I can follow my scale. I followed the scale Josh has to Earth. It's a very quick process and it only took a few moments. Unfortunately, if we don't know anyone where we are going, it is a little more difficult for us to get there and we must fly focusing on objects off in the distance and appearing at those and then refocusing. Much easier if you have given someone your scale. Takes days off a trip.'

He looked at Jazz for a long moment then stated, 'Here.' He reached up and pulled a scale from inside his forearm. Jazz winced slightly as he watched Whistle retrieve the scale. 'You can either carry my scale always but most find it easier just to consume it.'

Looking off into the distance, his eyes glazed over.

'Must go. Being sought. My hatchlings went to Sydney following another of my scales. Apparently the Whale has disturbing news regarding strange activities near your pole. Please give my regards to Josh. Had hoped I could say hello in person before I set off again. Will try and return soon.'

Whistle disappeared and Jason sat there for a few moments just staring at the spot Whistle had vacated.

'How wonderful to be able to fly and appear and disappear whenever you liked,' he mused out loud.

'So, my grandson, how was school?' Frieda asked. 'Oh and, if you like, I can show you how to crush that scale to powder and pop it over some food. Much more palatable than straight down. You've just received a very high dragon honour,' she said as she winked at Jason.

Jason told Frieda all about his day, including classes and the friends he'd made. He even included the incident involving the twins and the principal's car.

***

Walking into the gym with Brett, Jason noticed the area was predominantly wood, including wooden bleachers that ran down the longest sides facing each other. The area smelt faintly of a pine forest, which Jason assumed must be the result of some sort of wood maintenance. The main area of the gym housed an indoor basketball court with a stage at one end. Brett had told him that off to the sides of the stage there were a couple of change rooms for the drama club to use during performances. The gym floors were polished wood and the off-white walls were covered in flags and sporting banners.

They joined a group of students already waiting near the stage. Sally entered via a side door, talking loudly with another student. As she approached, she turned to Jason and Brett, rolling her eyes.

'Hi. Question. Would you prefer a snow theme or a Hawaiian theme?' asked her companion.

Taking her cue from the lack of any response, Sally jumped in. 'Hi. For those of you who don't know me, my name is Sally.'

'We know,' answered a shorter boy wearing large reading glasses that seemed almost too big for his face.

Smiling, Sally said, 'Thanks, Allan, and thanks to everyone for coming straight here after your last class. We are all here today to help plan and create a theme for our school dance. What Julia and I were discussing were themes. Did anyone have any suggestions?'

The group looked at each other, shrugging.

'Well, we have a lot of options,' continued Sally, 'but we only have a short time to plan so I was thinking a simple theme might be easier to organise, say a Hawaiian theme. People could dress in Hawaiian shorts and shirts and grass skirts. Maybe we could hire in a bunch of palm trees from a nursery to dress the room and a great big punch bowl.'

'Orrr,' said Julia, drawing out the word, 'we could create a winter wonderland with white snow and white balloons, white confetti could fall from the roof and we could crown a snow king and queen. After all, the hall is air-conditioned. It would feel like winter. We could ask Principal Walker to turn down the temperature and—' She stopped as the door slammed and two girls, a blonde wearing a blindfold and a brunette, entered, giggling.

'Sorry we're late,' said the brunette. 'We got a bit lost.'

'Lost?' inquired Allan. 'How do you get lost on the way to the school's only auditorium?'

'Carissa was practising being blind and I was helping her find her way. She has a project for heath and we have been evaluating the school's ability to service various disabilities.'

'Fine, fine,' said Julia. 'You're just in time to help decide the theme. Would you prefer a Winter Wonderland or a Hawaiian Theme?'

'Oooh, Hawaiian sounds fun,' replied Angela. Then, noticing Julia's frown. 'I mean, Winter Wonderland.'

'Oh great, sheep,' mumbled Brett.

Smiling, Angela shrugged and sat down.

'What about you, Carissa?' asked Julia. Carissa, having taken off her blindfold, looked around and shrugged too.

'What's happening?' asked Isabel. 'I can't see anything. It's so frustrating.'

After watching the scene intently, Jason jumped.

'How about we take a vote?' he suggested.

'And who are you?' asked Julia with a smile.

'Err, Jason.'

'Well, Jason, nice to meet you,' said Julia, 'I'm Julia.'

She walked over and perched herself next to Jason, so snugly that he was forced to move closer to Brett.

'Did anyone ever tell you you look almost exactly like Rupert Grint? Only taller,' she added tapping her chin and tilting her head.

'Yes, I believe I have heard that before. No, I don't believe we are related,' added Jason.

'So, a vote,' interrupted Sally. 'Great idea, Jason. Allan, could I borrow some pages from your notebook? Great, thanks. Pen please.'

Someone passed her a ballpoint pen.

'Excellent. Angela, Julia, Carissa, Brett, Allan, Jason, me and—' She looked up at the two remaining faces expectantly.

'Bonnie and Macka,' said the girl who had supplied the pen. 'It's short for Matilda but she hates that, so we call her Macka.'

'Great. Nine.' Tearing off bits of paper Sally handed a piece to everyone, and a pen to Macka. 'Write your preference on the paper and then scrunch it up and pop them in Brett's hat,' she said grabbing it off his head. Brett frantically ran fingers through his hair.

Not long after, Sally thrust the hat full of scrunched-up slips of paper at Jason. 'Jason, if you could do the honours.'

'Read aloud,' said Isabel. 'I'm tired of not being able to see anything properly. Would you mind talking more?'

Jason smiled. Poor Iz. He was sure she would have broken earlier.

'1 Winter Wonderland,' shouted Jason.

'Not deaf,' said Isabel and Brett in unison.

'Sorry,' said Jason.

'2 Hawaiian, 3 Hawaiian, 4 Winter, 5 Hawaiian, 6 Hawaiian, 7 Hawaiian and ...'

'Never mind,' said Sally. 'Hawaiian it is. It clearly has the most votes.'

'Yes,' said Julia. 'But I want to know what the last votes were.' She looked pointedly at Angela and Carissa.

'Not necessary,' said Sally, glancing at the relieved Angela as she swept up the tickets and dropped them in a nearby bin. 'So, tasks. We have six weeks in which to plan.'

'Hey, who made you boss?' asked Julia.

'All those in favour of Sally?' asked Brett.

Five hands shot up. Julia pouted, folding her arms.

***

'So, what's the VidComms for?' asked Jason.

'Stan says it's something to do with the Inkaba. Whistle is waiting at home as well,' replied Isabel.

They were on their way home after the school dance meeting and Isabel had let him know that his dad had called a video meeting.

'Hmm ... I wonder what they are up to?' pondered Jason.

'Who?' asked Sally and Brett, coming up behind him.

'Who were you talking to?' asked Sally.

'Me,' Jason went red, 'I was, I was—'

'Singing,' said Isabel in his ear.

'Singing,' Jason blurted out.

'Oh,' replied Brett.

'Thanks for voting for the Hawaiian theme, guys. Can't imagine a Winter Wonderland in the Territory. I mean I can imagine it, but does it make sense?'

'Yeah,' said Brett, 'I am not wearing a suit either. A Hawaiian shirt will do me fine.'

'What about you, Jason? Have you got some cool Hawaiian threads from the States?'

'I'm sure I'll find something,' replied Jason, somewhat distracted by his discussion with Isabel.

'Well, this is me. See you later,' Sally said waving as she walked off.

'Hey,' said Brett after they had walked on a bit, 'do you want to come over for dinner? Mum won't mind. Brad is at Jamie's tonight so we are one mouth down.'

'I'd love to,' replied Jason.

'You can't tonight,' said Isabel. 'You're expected at home.'

'I know,' said Jason.

'Know what?' said Brett.

'I mean I can't tonight. I have to go home. I promised my gran.'

'Oh, okay. Raincheck then.'

Jason looked at the sky, 'Nah, I don't think so. Not tonight.'

'What?' asked Brett. 'No, I meant another time. It's a saying. Don't you have rainchecks in the States? Oh, probably not. Okay, another time then, mate.'

'Great, see you tomorrow then.'

'Yeah, bye.'

'Farah, Walter's AI, says Walter and his daughter have just arrived as well,' Isabel informed Jason.

***

Faroon paced his book room. There was still time before the Keepers convened and he was formulating how to commence discussions.

At that moment, Alala walked in, carrying two cups of steaming Koor.

'So, how goes it, husband?'

'I have nothing good to tell them, Alala. I hope the other Keepers have something new to report in the meeting or suggestions. Would you like to stay for the discussions? Jazz will be in attendance when I call Earth, as will Walter, Josh and Frieda. Not the most opportune time for a family reunion but at least you will get to see him and know he is doing well. I'll call Dad last, then I can fill him in on the discussions we have had with the other Keepers.'

'Of course,' replied Alala, but she stayed to support her husband as much as to see her son.

***

Jason ran down the driveway to the house and saw Whistle, Josh, Frieda and Walter sitting on the porch with a young girl.

'Good. You're here,' boomed Josh, startling Whistle who promptly disappeared.

'Oops,' said Whistle as he reappeared. 'Scared the colour out of me.' He grinned.

A light, tinkling laugh followed from the young girl as she rocked back and forth, holding one knee up with her hands.

Josh raised his eyebrows at Whistle and then threw a weird half-grin at the young girl, more scary than reassuring. *Wow, he really needs to work on that,* thought Jason, realising for the first time his grandfather was actually really awkward with all kids, not just him.

'This is my daughter, Saranah, or Sarah as we call her here on Earth.'

'How do you do?' asked Jason.

'Well, thank you,' replied Sarah softly. 'And this is Dixie,' she announced politely holding up her necklace.

Isabel piped up. 'Hello, Mistress Sarah, Dixie. I am Isabel and Jason you have met.'

'Yes, yes,' said Josh. 'Now everyone knows each other. We have a few moments before Faroon calls. You may as well wait out here. Walter, can we speak? We have some things to discuss quickly.'

'I will get some refreshments then,' said Frieda.

'Can I help?' asked Sarah.

'Of course, come along.'

That left Whistle and Jason alone. 'How goes it, young Jason? Enjoying Earth still?'

'Absolutely,' replied Jason enthusiastically, 'and how is your scouting going?'

'Nothing so far. However, some wonderful sightseeing.'

'So, what did the Whales have to say? You went off to see them after your last visit.'

Jason had learnt about Whales. Large mammals. Incredibly intelligent beings, that lived and travelled the oceans.

Whistle frowned. 'The Whale said large ships come and kill his pod. They haul his kind from the water where they must live to survive; they pull them out with giant hooks. Soon after his family are on these boats, he says he can no longer feel them. Apparently, they are killed for scientific reasons even though science has already explored them in great depth. Look it up – it will be in your textbooks. When we have done with the scourge of the Inkaba, I will ask the Council of Keepers to answer their research questions somehow. The Whales will provide them with any information. They wish only to live in peace.'

Jason put his hand on Whistle's shoulder, a tear rolled down the dragon's cheek. 'I knew Marlow. Marlow was one they took.' By the time he finished, tears were streaming down his face.

'They are ready for us,' said Isabel sombrely.

'I am sorry for your loss,' said Jason.

'Me, too,' said Isabel.

Whistle ran the back of his scaly hand across his eyes. 'Thank you both. I should have known sooner but it is not often I visit Earth these days. I should have come sooner. Marlow was one hundred and fifty Earth years. He had many more left,' he said, smiling grimly at Jason. 'Come. If we don't hurry, there could be more deaths than just Marlow. Some planets take millennia to recover from these aliens.

Whistle, waddling towards the back door with his stumpy tail swinging from side to side, suddenly looked up at Jason, a grin spreading across his face.

'Want to try some magic, Jason?'

'Sure.'

'Grab my hand.'

Disappearing then reappearing near a couch. This must be the study, thought Jason.

Walter and Josh didn't blink. They were no doubt used to Whistle's tricks – Jason not so. He sat down hard on the couch, a bewildered smile playing on his face.

'Jazz!' His mother's voice startled him from his reverie.

'Mum!'

Projecting on a wall was an image of his mum and dad in his father's book room.

'Mum, Dad,' said Jason.

'Son,' said Josh. 'Alala. How are you?'

'Well, thanks. You and Mum?' replied Alala

'Good,' replied Josh.

'Walter,' said Faroon, acknowledging his friend.

'Faroon, Alala, how are you?'

'Whistle, how are you? How are the hatchlings?'

'Running around Earth somewhere, but they aren't much like hatchlings now. Teenage browns, the last lot now. Their uncles watch them.'

Vanishing suddenly, Whistle reappeared on the screen in front of Jason next to his parents.

'Seemed more room over here,' said Whistle. 'I would have brought you too Jason, if I could, but takes more energy to jump far. Simpler on your own,' he finished with a sheepish smile and a shrug.

Frieda entered, carrying a tray of drinks and sandwiches.

'Sarah has just gone to play with Sam. She and Dixie are going to keep watch for any Inkaba trying to land in the backyard. I said she could take a look in your shuttle, Jason. I hope you don't mind. Dixie will make sure she doesn't touch anything she shouldn't.'

Jason shrugged, not minding either way.

'Mother,' said Faroon.

'Oh, you're here,' said Frieda turning. Beaming at the screen. 'Alala, don't you look beautiful? Where did you get that shade of silk? It's just beautiful. Whistle, aren't you lucky, you little devil? If I could just pop over there to see my son at a moment's notice like you, I would be the happiest mother on Earth.'

'Ahem,' Josh cleared his throat, in order to draw attention back to the purpose of the meeting.

'Yes, yes, of course,' said Frieda, settling herself on the couch next to Jason. Walter sat next to Frieda while Josh remained at his desk.

'So, Son, what is the news?'

'Not good, I am afraid, Father. Since those Inkaba troops left the other morning, no-one has caught sight of them again. We have also become aware that our communication with Master Olin has been lost. We no longer have any eyes or ears in their camp; we are completely blind to where they are going.

43

We briefed the other Keepers earlier but I just wanted you to hear from me the news about Olin.' He finished, suddenly looking very tired. Frieda put her hand out as if to comfort her son, then, realising he was just an image on a screen, she let it drop.

'You are doing a good job, Son.'

Faroon looked down. 'We lost contact a couple of days ago with our other spies as well. The elders can't feel the scales. They may be dead or captured. Maybe they remain undiscovered. If they have been caught, they might be cloaking. Let's hope.'

Everyone nodded in agreement.

'So, Whistle,' said Faroon, turning to his side. 'Any news from your scouts?'

'No, none as yet,' Whistle replied with a sigh. Jason knew he was thinking of his friends, the Whales. 'They will soon head off to other planets to help with their searches. I stay and watch with a smaller number.'

'Good. Dad, have you alerted the other Micoronians on Earth?'

'Yes, Son. As soon as we spoke the other night I sent out correspondence and skyped most in the code.'

'Good. Our troops and resources remain vigilant. The 1st Armun has spoken to all the other heads of planets in nearby systems and within a sixty-day transport radius. With their numbers, the Inkaba will only travel a month or two but that still gives them much scope and us much distance to warn. I wanted to speak to you today to remind you of the great urgency of our mission. All must remain vigilant. With so many already en route, they will soon set the scene for others to follow. They will move shortly. Jason, keep your eyes open, Son. Even the slightest hint of something strange, I need to know.' Alala knew the unspoken end of his sentence ... *that you are safe.*

'Yes, sir, of course,' replied Jason straightening a little more in his seat.

'I'm sorry I cannot give you more information. No other Keeper had any new information. I will relay any news as I receive it. Take care, my family.'

The transmission ended.

'Well,' said Josh, 'we had thought we might have more than a couple of months but, with their troops already on the move, it means they will send for the rest of their clan as soon as they have established a base and … destroyed or captured any opposition. We must remain alert.'

'I agree,' said Walter. 'We have people of Micoron in every state of Australia and a number spread throughout the world. Whistle, your team will monitor what we miss with the help of your Whale friends. We have good scouts here. Let's hope the other planets are being as vigilant.'

***

'That was great,' said Walter. Everyone had enjoyed generous portions of lasagne prepared by Frieda.

'Agreed,' said Whistle, rubbing his full belly.

'Should we adjourn to the lounge with our Koor?' asked Freida.

From there they took turns sharing stories about their Earth adventures.

Sarah, Jason discovered, attended primary school in the central business district. They had lived on Earth close to five Earth years. She travelled back to Micoron every second year to learn more about Micoron and visit her mother. Sarah's mother had divorced Walter when Sarah was two. Her mother had remarried and now had a new family with two sisters for Saranah.

Jason also learned that Sarah carried an unusual gift. Able to see snippets of the future, she had foreseen the death of her father in one such possible future. Only she could avert his death, so it was decided she must remain near him on Earth.

Frieda and Josh had spent considerable time on Earth travelling around Australia in a caravan and exploring various countries. As Micoron was able to fabricate Earth's precious stones relatively easily, they had sold a small number and invested the money in shares that paid reasonable returns. This enabled them to sustain a comfortable lifestyle.

It was ten o'clock. As Walter stood to leave, Sarah, who had been asleep on the rug on the floor, woke up. She stared unblinkingly at Jason. Cocking her head to one side she smiled, saying, 'You will save him.'

'What? Save who?' asked Jason. He paused. 'Save who?' he said louder.

Focusing on Jason, the clouded look disappeared from Sarah's eyes.

Yawning and stretching, she finally noticed everyone staring at her.

'What? Oh, did I dream, Daddy?' she asked, looking at Walter.

'Yes, sweetheart. You told Jason he would need to save someone. Do you know who he will save, Sarah?'

Frowning, she shook her head, 'Sorry.'

Walter turned to Jason. 'Her gift has different levels. She can see things sometimes like they have just happened; other times she dreams but needs to remain in that trance to be able to answer you. If she wakes completely she will often forget. Never mind. If it is important she will dream it again one day. Her grandmother also had a similar gift as a child. As they get older, I am told, they grow out of the visions, but Sarah's still seem to have a lot of strength. I will let you know, Josh, if she says more.'

'Sorry, Son,' he said, turning back to Jason, 'it can be a little unsettling to be in one of her visions. Trust me, I know.'

'Come, Sarah. Time for home and bed, honey.'

Taking her father's hand and waving goodbye, she looked at Jason for an extra moment before smiling and turning to follow Walter.

'Strange,' thought Jason. 'Save who?'

He wondered how often her visions came true.

'Bye,' said Whistle but vanished before Jason could get out his, 'Goodnight.'

***

Sarah dreamt the same dream that night. Jason with his four friends. He would save him. Sarah woke smiling. She had known she would dream again, but she would not tell her father. Too much information about one's future was not good.

Having listened to a number of the stories recounted that evening, she had eventually got sleepy, dozing off on the rug. Her father had told everyone about his potential death in her visions. Once again she felt the stabbing guilt in her gut for lying. Her mother had remarried but her father had not. She refused to leave him on his own. So, at an early age she had lied. One day, when she was older, she would explain her lie, but not today, as she would be forced to live with her mother and, while she missed her every day, she would not leave Walter alone.

Sarah came from a long line of seers. Her power grew stronger every year. It would not pass after childhood. The Dragon Elders had confirmed that for her. She could not control all of what she witnessed or whose lives she saw, but she was getting better at controlling the dreams in order to repeat them.

Rolling over to check the clock, she realised there were still a few hours before dawn. Closing her eyes, she was soon dreaming of dragons playing with unicorns on a land covered in thick green forests. A big black stream flowed nearby and where they played, green hills met purple skies showcasing two huge moons. Sarah loved dreaming of the dragons' world and often they would accompany her in her dreams. They would show off their planet and its many beautiful places to rest. Sometimes they would play games of skill. Sometimes she would discuss her gifts with Dragon Elders and other times they would just lie in the sun and bask together while the dragons recounted stories from the ancient past.

Chapter 6 – Fate

'Morning, Iz. Standby. Well?' asked Jason rubbing sleep from his eyes.

'Actually, no. Whistle came and borrowed me. He needed someone to get into the computers that operate Earth's satellites. I told him you wouldn't mind. We have now set up a link that allows me to see what's going on everywhere, all the time.'

'Have you learnt anything interesting so far?' asked Jason. Noticing his ring wasn't on his finger, he wondered how on earth he had not felt the ring being taken off.

'It's wonderful, Jason. I can see everything. I finally have my eyes back. There is so much information to process that Stan and Dixie are helping. Your grandfather isn't keen on us all being patched in, in case we get picked up by their various scans, but I am managing to act like approved software. It's fun. I'm the only one connected. Stan and Dixie are just processing what I send them.'

Jason laughed, hearing the excitement in Isabel's voice.

'Stan kept an eye on you last night. You didn't move much – must have been very tired. Ready for today? Let's go to the fete. I can't wait to see what everyone looks like'.

She nudged him along by running a mild current through the ring he had just picked up off his side table and put on.

He hummed in the shower and through most of his morning chores – even while running the scraps out to the chickens and grabbing the eggs. Then it was time to mow the lawns on the ride-on mower.

'Isabel, some tunes, please. Something local would be good. Let's get me more in tune with what everyone else listens to around here.'

'How's this?'

'Brilliant!'

***

Sally and Brett were waiting at the top of their street. They had organised to walk to the fete together, and later they planned to catch a bus into town to see a movie and grab dinner. Frieda would pick them up after dinner.

The school fete had been organised by students to raise additional money for their upcoming school trip.

'Wow, she is very pretty,' whispered Isabel in Jason's ear. 'What an amazing shade of blue.'

Looking up at a bird, Sally was dressed in a yellow summer frock that reached her ankles, with white thongs on her tanned feet. Her hair hung loose past her shoulders and, for the first time, Jason noticed it reached halfway down her back. Her eyes, he realised, were the colour of the ocean. They reminded Jason of looking at Earth from space.

He was staring so intently at Sally that she cleared her throat for the second time and clicked her fingers in his face.

'Am I wearing something of yours?' challenged Sally, a grin on her face and a slight blush. Brett snickered, punching him in the arm.

'Come on then, Romeo,' said Brett.

'What ... oh,' stammered Jason, 'I wasn't ... um ... Iz said and I was just trying to ... oh, never mind.'

His two friends burst out laughing, making Jason blush even more.

As he walked on, Jason mused. He had known Brett and Sally for almost a month now and often felt completely at ease with them, and then there were other times when he felt a bit I like an alien – an orange-headed, tall, uncoordinated alien.

***

The fete spread out across the school oval. A mishmash of colourful tents and shade structures with food trucks scattered throughout. People milled around the colourful tents, others chatted under big trees at the edges of the oval. It was hot and muggy. A ball throwing game, near the centre of the field, attracted a small crowd.

'I'm going to sink that Home Ed teacher Ms Wilder for flunking us last semester,' announced Brad loudly to Jamie. Ms Wilder was currently perched on a long board, her legs dangling over a large water tank. A line of kids took turns throwing a hard ball at a lever to the left of the cage.

Jamie and Brad waved at Sally, Jason and Brett. Sally, raising her hand slightly in acknowledgement, firmly steered the boys in the other direction.

'After all,' she said as if answering their question, 'we are still in Ms Wilder's class this semester and I, for one, would rather not attract the same grades as your brother and his mate.'

The boys didn't respond but Brett smiled sheepishly as they continued to the cake stand.

'Hi, Kai,' said Sally. 'We are here to help. What can we do?'

Kai, a tall student of Asian appearance, had joined them from Singapore at the start of the year. With long black hair, green eyes and some of the best grades in the school, Kai should be popular but she came across as shy and Jason had noticed that she didn't really seem to hang out with anyone in particular.

'Hi,' replied Kai quietly, just nodding at the boys with a small smile. 'I can stay here if you want to go and enjoy the fete. I don't mind.'

'What?' asked Jason before anyone else had a chance, even though he wasn't rostered to work on the stall anyway. 'This looks like fun but why would you want to stay in here all day?' gesturing towards the red and yellow tent and the white trestle table laden with cakes, toffees and other treats made by the students in Ms Wilder's class.

'Surely you would like Ms Wilder to take a dip, or there's the talent show or a few rides about by the looks of things,' he said, squinting off towards the rides. 'We could go and sit in the little planes that go in circles or those chairs that sort of fly out.' He spread his arms wide with this last statement, mimicking the motion of the chair ride.

Without realising he had invited Kai to hang out with him.

'Sure. Brett and I will mind the fort. You two go and have fun.' It was Sally who responded, pushing Brett towards the far side of the table. Then she poked him in the ribs and nodded her head in Kai's direction.

'Yes, of course. Go with Jason. He's sure to find something fun for you to do.'

Kai looked like she was going to protest. But Brett and Sally stood firmly behind the counter nodding, smiling and waving. Jason smiled, a bit bemused when he realised he had just asked his first girl out – unintentionally of course. He thought about his mates back home. Some of them dated at this age but nothing serious. A trip to watch a sporting game or lunch, maybe a dance.

Astute Isabel piped up in his ear. 'Get her to look around. I want to see this first date.' There was amusement in her voice as she teased him about his unintentional date.

As the two of them walked off, Brett shouted, 'Don't be more than a couple of hours, though. Someone should come and cover our shift then so we can all go grab a bite together and maybe get in a few activities before we have to go.'

'Sure,' said Jason. With that he turned to Kai. 'So, does "Kai" mean something?'

Kai blushed again, looking around nervously, tucking her hair behind her ears.

'I am sorry. Did I ask something wrong?' asked Jason.

'No, no. It's okay. Kai is mostly a boy's name. It means *rejoice*,' she said, shrugging. 'I was supposed to be a boy. Luckily some girls are still called Kai too'

'Oh, cool,' said Jason, not sure what else to say. 'So, is there anything here you wanted to do?'

They stopped at a row of colourful tents to watch a game. Players scored points after placing a ball in a clown's mouth. Each ball would settle in a slot with a number. Contestants then added up all the numbers their balls had landed on in the hope of receiving the prize that corresponded to that number. In the next tent was a wall of balloons that players threw darts at.

'Roll up, roll up,' spruiked the man in front of this game. 'Win the lady a prize, sir? All you have to do is throw these darts at a balloon and behind every balloon is a number that might win you a prize. Hit the right balloon and she could be going home with a jumbo teddy or giant elephant. Roll up, roll up.'

Jason reached into his pocket for some change.

'Wait,' said Isabel in his ear, 'let me watch for a minute.' Jason flattened his hand on his thigh so Isabel could watch. 'You need to hit the balloons across the bottom. They are the most likely to host the major prizes as they are at the level of young children who often don't have good aim.'

'Excuse me,' said Jason, 'I'll have a go.' After a couple of practice, mock throws Jason smiled sheepishly at Kai, before getting down on his knees. He threw each dart given to him, hitting three balloons in a row. The darts had been weighted wrong to hinder the contestant's aim. But this game was not unlike Paton at home where you intentionally attached various weights to small knives that you then threw at a target. So Jason knew how to adjust his aim.

'You have a couple of winners there, laddie,' said the young man in front of the stalls. 'With your score, you can pick one prize from this top row and one from here.'

Both rows contained large stuffed animals. Jason turned to Kai.

'Is there something you would like? I am not really into stuffed animals. Pick something for Sally too then we can wander back and get them to mind them for us.'

Kai chose a lion for herself and a panda-shaped animal for Sally. Both were cute and furry in a cheap, side-show-animal way. The lion was half the size of Kai so Jason carried the Panda back for Sally.

Once they had discarded the toys – much to the excitement of Sally, who declared she loved hers and named him Shadow – Jason and Kai set off again to enjoy the fete.

'Where to now?'

'I don't mind. Wherever you would like to go.'

'Nah, come on. Surely there's something you were hoping to see while you were here.'

Kai hesitated, then shrugged.

'Ah-ha. There is something. Come on. We have plenty of time. I want to see the talent show. Apparently, Brad is performing something crazy with Jamie but that's not till later and, if we miss it, I am sure they will replay it for us. So, what is it?'

'There are a couple of basketball games on today and I was hoping to watch for a bit.'

'Basketball?' queried Jason.

'They throw a ball through a hoop,' said Isabel.

'Oh, basketball, of course. Let's go then.'

He remembered something about basketball from his Earth studies – but only the basics, there were two hoops and two teams maybe?

***

'Wow! What a great game,' Jason enthused.

They had watched an exhibition match of boys and girls teams. At half-time they'd chosen people from the audience to shoot from the three-point line to win one of two hampers filled with homemade treats. Kai had been chosen first and had made the shot straight up. A couple of other guys had been chosen before Jason and missed but when he got a go he also made the shot.

As they stood up to leave they were approached by both captains.

'So,' it was the guy who spoke first, 'was that a fluke shot or do you think you could do it again?'

'How about you?' asked the female captain. 'Do you play?'

'Not sure,' replied Jason. 'I could give it another go.' Walking off towards the hoop with the captain, Jason dropped the ball in the hoop nine out of ten attempts. At the other end of the court Kai performed impressively.

'Well,' said Jason, 'it seems they want me to continue playing this game.'

'Me too,' Kai said beaming.

'Great. My name is Grant. Can you both make it to training Tuesday nights? We play Thursday nights.'

Kai looked worried, but Jason piped up for both of them.

'Of course.'

'Great,' said the girl's captain. 'I'm Maria. I'll see you on Tuesday then.'

'Do we meet here?' Jason asked

'Actually, we train in the auditorium. Do you know where that is?' Kai and Jason nodded.

Walking away, each carrying a hamper, Kai turned to Jason. 'I'm not sure my dad will let me.'

'What do you mean, Kai? Of course, he will. It's healthy exercise. Besides, you have to teach me the rules, I have no idea about the game. I picked up a bit from watching but I don't want to look lame. We'll get Sally's dad to speak to your dad if he has a problem with it,' said Jason offhandedly.

Kai paused then smiled. 'Okay,' she said.

Jason, realising what he had just promised, hoped that Sally would be able to back him on this one.

'Should we go get Sally and Brett before the talent show?' asked Kai.

Nodding, Jason added. 'Hey, do you want to come to the movies with us later too?'

'That would be nice, but the basketball might be enough to ask my dad's permission for today. He doesn't like me going places without him and after-school activities that don't involve chess club may not go over too well either. I was lucky to be allowed to come here today. My mother helped get me to this one, plus I said I was being graded on it for home economics, which is sort of true. We have to report on our fundraising activities,' she added weakly.

***

'Oh, my goodness, too funny,' Sally said wiping tears from her eyes, with her index fingers.

Roars of laughter continued to erupt from those watching the talent show.

Jamie and Brad were performing a talking-belly routine of the principal and Ms Wilder hosting a cooking show. They had covered their heads and shoulders with large cardboard hats and had cut-out paper outfits of shirts and trousers that hung below faces painted on their bellies. They were using their belly button as the character's mouth and moved it with their hands to talk. Jason was laughing so hard he snorted the melted part of his ice cup out his nose. Kai laughed, visibly relaxing for the first time.

After their act, Jamie and Brad joined them on the grass to watch the rest of the performances on stage. They took it upon themselves to critique each act as if they were judges. They marked the good acts down considerably and were constantly referring back to the great act performed earlier involving the principal and Ms Wilder and how it was the sure-fire favourite.

After the show, they all walked Kai to the car park where her parents were picking her up.

Jason spoke first. 'Great to meet you, Kai.'

'Yeah,' said Brad. 'You should totally hang with us more often'

Sally walked the last bit to the carpark with Kai. The boys waited under a tree a little bit further back at Kai's request. Not supposed to talk to boys, she warned them she would never be allowed out again if all four walked her to her parents' car, especially the twins. Brad's reputation, it seemed, had preceded him and would not impress her parents. Sally, on the other hand, might gain her some bonus points and Kai hoped to mention basketball to her parents with Sally there. After all, having the principal's daughter reinforce the idea wouldn't hurt either – especially with her dad.

A few minutes later, Kai's parents arrived. Sally spoke to them briefly, waved goodbye to Kai and made her way back to the boys.

'Well?' It was Jason who questioned Sally as soon as she returned to the group.

'She gets to try out, at least,' said Sally, 'as long as her grades don't slip and she agrees to go and visit her grandmother this Christmas. Wow! Talk about a strict dad who throws in a little bit of blackmail to boot. Her mum has invited me around for tea, which sounds decidedly English, but Kai assures me it's Chinese tea and includes some yummy dumplings and spring rolls.'

'Cool. When are we going?' asked Jamie.

'Nope. Don't think you boys were invited.'

'What do you mean? Jason spent all afternoon with Kai. Surely he gets to go,' said Brett, winking.

Sally put her hand over Brett's face and pushed him back gently. 'Sorry, Jason, but you're a boy.'

'Yeah, I know.'

'So must be time to go, hey kids? said Brad.

'Wait. You're not coming, are you?' asked Brett. 'Did Mum say you could? Aren't you still grounded?'

'Nope. I think I was driving her nuts being under her feet all the time. She basically made me and Jamie promise to stay out of trouble and then removed the grounding. Hey, but we are going to try and be good for a while. Mum wasn't mad at us this time. She just looked really tired. So, what are we going to see?'

They bumped into Josh and Frieda as they were leaving and loaded them up with the Panda and the hamper. Josh shook the boys' hands and Frieda offered them all peanut brittle before reconfirming the pickup arrangements and waving goodbye as the group headed for the bus shelter.

***

'It's just a movie. Nothing to worry about. Not real,' consoled Iz through Jason's earpiece. Always monitoring his vitals, she had picked up Jason's elevated heart rate as he watched the movie.

The movie's storyline involved an alien race with massive ships that came to take over Earth. In the end, Earth triumphed, but not before many had died and cities had been destroyed.

'Not real at this stage, anyway,' added Jason under his breath.

'What an awesome movie.' It was Brad

'Brilliant,' replied Jamie.

'I'm not sure Sally saw it,' chimed in Brett. 'She spent three quarters of it hiding behind me or her hands,' he grinned.

'Are you alright, mate?' Brad had noticed Jason's face.

'You look positively green,' added Brett.

'Did you eat something bad? Are you feeling alright?' asked Sally. 'Here, sit down and have some water.'

'Yeah,' said Jason shaking his head. 'Yeah, I'm fine.'

'Motion sickness,' said Isabel in his ear. 'You have motion sickness.'

'Motion sickness,' repeated Jason. 'Everything kept moving too much. My eyes couldn't take everything in,' he lied. It was not something he suffered from having often flown at light speed and having spent heaps of time in little cruisers

56

that felt every bump. It was not a trait found on his planet. There were rarely any cases of motion sickness reported on Micoron and, if there were, an implant provided by the medical staff usually counteracted it – no-one had to suffer.

'I'm better now.'

'Good. Are we ready for dinner?' asked Jamie, rubbing his belly.

Jason noticed his gran already waiting for them.

'I forgot to tell you,' said Isabel. 'The movie went for three hours. Your time's up.'

'Guys did you know that was a three-hour movie?' asked Jason. 'Gran, we haven't eaten anything yet.'

'Oh, you haven't? Would you like to go have something to eat? Or we can always whip something up for you at home. I have a rather large roast in the oven. We can call and get Josh to pop the temperature up. There will be plenty for all of you. Your grandfather is going out so it'll be nice to have a full house.'

Saturday evenings his grandfather taught English at one of the local schools. It was for adults learning English as a second language. His grandfather could speak a number of alien languages fluently, including some earth dialects, so he volunteered his time once a week.

'Roast, I love roast,' stated Jamie climbing into the LandCruiser. 'I'll take home cooking any day.'

Laughing, they followed Jamie into the car.

Frieda pulled Jason aside. 'Jason, Josh has already gone. Tell Isabel to get Stan to flick the oven up will you. At least that will get things started and we can pop the veggies in when we get home. Lucky I put the roast on. I actually ran out of time and forgot to turn it up before I realised I had to come and get you.'

In the car Jason and Sally handled the introductions. The boys, being polite, gave Sally the front seat. She chatted to Frieda all the way home while the boys discussed aliens.

'I would have known earlier about the invasion and would have intercepted them in my starcruiser. I would have blown up that mother ship earlier too,' stated Jamie.

'Now does anyone need to call their parents and let them know about the change of plans?' asked Frieda. 'You're welcome to use my phone. Jason just grab it out of the top of my bag will you?'

Dinner was ready within 40 minutes of them getting home, thanks to some early intervention from Stan in the kitchen. Everyone tucked into the lamb roast, with homegrown pumpkin, sweet potato and spuds. Jamie impressed everyone with his cauliflower au gratin – something he had learnt in home economics the day Brad had been home sick.

'So, which one of you two is it that leads the other astray?' asked Frieda, smiling. Jason had told his grandmother about his new friends, including his first day with Jamie and Brad sitting in the office.

'I'm the brains. He's the brawn,' stated Jamie with a smirk.

'Na ah,' replied Brad. 'He's the ...' He paused, realising he was just about to say Jamie was the stronger. Winking at Jason, he continued, 'Actually, I'm the brains and the brawn,' he stated, kissing his bicep in mock body-builder style.

Laughing, they each got up, carrying something from the table to the kitchen.

'Now, who's for some dessert? There is a wonderfully wicked trifle I prepared earlier in the fridge. Would anyone like some?' asked Frieda.

'Yes,' they said in unison, except for Sally who added a 'please'.

'Good then. How about a couple of you start on that washing-up and then Sally ... Jamie you can give me a hand with dessert?'

'The twins' mum is here,' announced Isabel to Jason. Just as he looked up, there was a knock at the door.

'Hello,' the twins' mum said, opening the screen door. 'I'm Mona, mother to these two terrors,' and, pointing at Jamie, 'as well as that adopted one there.'

'Mona ... Frieda. Nice to meet you. We were just getting to dessert. Won't you join us, then I can smuggle in a couple of adult cups of coffee to go with the trifle.'

'If you're sure you have enough. I have just left the girls with their father and a cup of coffee and dessert all for me sounds like heaven. They haven't been too much trouble have they? Going from one to five is usually a little overwhelming.'

'They have all been wonderful, actually. They're more than welcome to come over any time. It's nice to have all the noise in the house.'

'Good, excellent,' replied Mona, eyeing Brad and Jamie suspiciously.

***

Mona took Sally, too, dropping her off on the way home. It was a late night. After dessert they had all sat down in front of the television to watch a few funny soaps. Well, they half-watched and laughed and half-talked over them as they drank hot chocolate. Mona and Frieda chatted as well, organising to meet up the following day to visit the local markets together.

'What a nice night. Mona is a very patient and kind woman with four of her own and, the way she talks about Jamie, you would think he was hers too. Now, are you ready for bed? Its Sunday tomorrow, another full day to get up to some mischief. Leave the mugs. I'll wash them tomorrow.'

'Night then, Gran.'

'Goodnight Jason, sleep well.'

***

'Whistle wants to know if he can visit,' Isabel said as Jason was entering his room. He hadn't quite started to undress or get into his pyjamas.

'Sure,' replied Jason. Whistle appeared as the word was spoken.

'Master Jazz, are you well?' asked Whistle. 'I thought I would see if you were free tomorrow. I have surveillance jobs. Thought you might like to tag along. Did you bring accor jacket? You will need one; it's cool and wet where we are going. Soft shoes and accor pants too if you have them.' Jason was glad he had his jacket – accor clothing kept the wearer cool or hot depending on the outside temperature.

'Sounds great. I'll just need to ask Frieda.'

'No need,' said Whistle. 'I asked her on the way in. I was with Stan when he asked Isabel if I could visit.'

'Can you make sure he is ready by 7.00 am, Iz?'

'Of course,' replied Isabel.

'Good,' said Whistle, vanishing.

Chapter 7 – A Spectacular Meeting

Whistle arrived at 6.55 am. Jason was sitting on his bed, his jacket tied around his waist, runners on his feet. 'Where are we going, Whistle?' he asked.

'To see the Whales, of course. The mighty Migram is passing as her pod makes their Southern migration back to the Antarctic to feed for the summer months. I thought you might like to meet Migram and hear about some of her travels. Are you ready?'

'Yes. Do I need anything else?'

Whistle gave Jason the once over. 'No, but just give me a second. I will come back for you but we will have to move fast or your raft will float away.'

'Raft? Why do I need a raft?'

Whistle cocked his head. 'Because you don't have wings.' With that he vanished.

Re-appearing, he grabbed Jason's hand and they both vanished. Appearing again above a yellow plastic inflatable boat that Jason landed in softly after letting go of Whistle's hand. The sun, bright overhead, was teamed with a cold wind. Quickly pulling his waterproof accor jacket from around his waist, Jason slipped it on and zipped it up. Looking around he took note of his surroundings. He was in a raft in the middle of a beautiful deep blue ocean, with a pale blue sky overhead – no land in sight.

'Put on that life jacket too, please,' ordered Whistle pointing to a bright orange vest in the boat. 'I don't want to explain to your grandfather, or any of your family for that matter, that I lost you in the Pacific Ocean.'

Jason obeyed. He was a little bewildered finding himself dumped in a little rocking boat in the open ocean, so did not respond.

'Are you ready to meet Migram?'

Nodding, Jason gazed out over the beautiful blue waters.

A cry, 'Eeeeeeaae,' came from Whistle.

Instantly, in the distance, a large dark creature rose up almost completely out of the water except for its tail, stayed there, momentarily suspended, before crashing back into the water on its side, sending up a large spray and disappearing back into the blue.

'She sees us. Here she comes,' cried Whistle excitedly.

Jason let out a big breath, half-scared, half-excited, as the dark figure approached.

'Of course,' Whistle said, as if holding a conversation. 'Jason, Migram has given you permission to touch her side. She will then be able to hear you and you her. She says she senses fear. Are you scared, Jason? Do not be afraid. Migram does not eat people – only krill, plankton, small fish.' He marked these off on his claws as he spoke each word. 'You don't look like any of these so you will be fine,' said Whistle, winking.

Relax, he told himself as a large dark eye appeared beside the boat. Slowly reaching out his hand, he touched the beautiful dark skin of the Whale. It was wet but smooth, a bit like wet rubber.

'Heelllllooo, Jasssooon,' a soft feminine voice echoed in his head. 'Wheee have beeeen waiting to meeett you.'

A smaller dark figure appeared beside the boat.

'Hi,' said a small whispery voice in Jason's head. 'I'mmm Natt.'

Laughing, Jason relaxed. Natt was a small version of Migram – a much smaller version.

'This issh Nathor,' the female voice in his head spoke again, 'she is my calf.'

'Pleased to meet you both,' said Jason, finding his voice.

Jason and Whistle spent the morning chatting with Migram and Natt. Natt's thoughts – a jumble of images from eating to watching dolphins. She broke these up with somersaults and spins, swimming around her mother and exploring – but never too far off.

Migram, Jason and Whistle discussed the weather and what they had seen, which wasn't anything too suspicious. Migram showed concern as she reported on ice caps melting in the Antarctic. Noting that, while it meant more oceans for her family, she worried that it would unbalance things. Without the ice to reflect the sun, the Earth would attract more heat, warming the planet and changing

Earth's weather patterns, which would in turn affect food production and where people could live. 'Will they try and live on the sea?' she asked Whistle.

Whistle and Migram discussed this at great length. What if the Council of Keepers interfered and helped these Earthlings? What would be the repercussions? What would they do first? Neither Migram nor Whistle thought it appropriate for the Keepers to interfere; they just seemed to be enjoying the discussion as to what could be. Sharing ideas on what technology the Keepers might give the humans and the possible chain of events that would follow.

Just as Jason was beginning to get hungry, Migram decided she should go. She advised Jason she could feel his hunger pains and he was making both Natt and herself very hungry. She was ready to go off and find some food, as Natt had begun feeding on her milk and this was compounding her hunger. She wished Whistle and Jason well and told them to come visit again soon; she had more philosophy to discuss with Whistle and wanted to hear more about his family. She would be somewhere along the coast for another few months until reaching their feeding destination. As always, all Whistle needed to do was to seek his scale.

***

They appeared back at the house just as his grandfather was pulling up in his LandCruiser. Whistle decided to land outside in the sun so they could both warm up a bit.

'Whistle, Jason,' said Josh, nodding at each. 'You two were out early.'

'Yes,' replied Whistle, 'we have been with Migram and her new calf Nathor.'

'How fares Migram and her new cub?' asked Josh, suddenly interested. 'Was Orica with them?'

'No,' replied Whistle quietly, 'just Migram and Natt. Orica ...' he paused and looked down sadly. 'Orica was taken by whalers; they took Marlow too.'

'Oh, Whistle, that's terrible,' said Frieda coming out of the house. 'When? Why didn't you say something? Their barbaric hunting season has been finished for months.'

Josh had slumped down at the table and was staring off into space.

'I did not wish to upset you. I was told the night we spoke to your son. Things already seemed so full of doom and gloom, I did not wish to add to your worries. I hadn't been back for a while and we had not heard from Orica for a few months, but that is not unusual. I was to speak to her this visit.'

'Whistle, let's go inside and talk,' said Josh, his shoulders rounded. It seemed a chore for him to push himself up from the seat.

Watching them go, Frieda motioned Jason to sit at the outside table. As he sat, she started to explain the history of Orica and the Whales. 'Orica is the mother of Migram, who is always the mother of Natt, who is always the mother of Orica.'

'What?' said Jason bewildered.

'There are only three names given to female Whales: Orica, mother of water, Migram, mother of soil and Nathor, mother of the sky. All female Whales have one of these three names so Orica is always the mother of Migram, who is always the mother of Nathor, who is always the mother of Orica.'

'Oh,' said Jason thinking about it for a minute. 'Then what if they have more than one Whale calf?'

'Then they will be Nathor too. The rules still apply.'

'How do they tell each other apart?'

Frieda smiled. 'The same way you recognise your mother, even if you did not know her by the name "mother" – by voice and smell maybe.' She paused a minute before she continued her story. 'Josh was very close to Orica; they have known each other for many years. Your grandfather was hoping to spend some time with Orica over Christmas with some short trips to Antarctica with Whistle. Josh will be saddened by this loss. Orica had lived on this planet for years, she was the keeper of much information and wisdom. Hopefully, all of it has been shared with Migram. Anyway, enough chatter, you must be starving. Come, let's go make your grandfather and Whistle something to eat. We might have some mince to make hamburgers with. I am sure Whistle would prefer just the raw meat so it's really only us we need to cook for.'

The memories of his visit with Migram and Natt often returned to Jason over the next couple of weeks. He wished he could go and visit them again. Thinking of Natt and his somersaults made him smile, but Whistle hadn't come back to visit and Jason didn't want to interrupt him from scouting duties. He knew he must be busy. He also wondered what male Whales are called if female Whales only had three names. He knew Whistle's male Whale friend had been called Marlow.

***

You could feel the excitement in the air. The school dance was this Friday and each week the school camp to Central Australia got closer. Students had raised all costs for parents and teachers to travel plus $100 towards the cost of travel for each of the twenty-nine students going to Alice Springs. Language students had already travelled to their respective countries of study, so it was only those students not studying a language that would go to Alice Springs.

In an effort to raise more funds, the Year 8s had invited the two years above them to the dance, to bolster numbers and door sales. They had planned a small refreshment stand for the night and Sally had already volunteered both Jason and Brett's time at the stand.

Jason also had basketball this Thursday and he was looking forward to beating the Titans. The Titans had beaten his school the last couple of times they had played and, most recently, one of their team had knocked over Grant's brother who had broken his arm in the fall. Jason was now playing centre position in his place. His unusual height aided him in his jump shots and three pointers so the Jacobs Jaguars were looking forward to a competitive game with the chance of a win.

'Well,' said Sally.

'Well, what?' asked Brett.

They were walking home from school. Jason had had practice but Brett and Sally had been working on the decorations while he trained so they still all got to walk home together.

'Do you want to come over for dinner?'

'What, are you crazy? Dinner at the principal's house?' gasped Brett in mock horror, as Sally shoved him sideways.

'Yeah, why not?' said Brett. 'I was going to have to walk you home anyway. It's getting dark.'

'It's not dark, and why would you have to walk me home?'

'What about you, Jazz, coming?' asked Brett. Sally continued talking in the background about how sexist and unnecessary Brett's comments were, spouting off about women who had proved themselves stronger and better at defending themselves than men.

'Nah, mate, gotta go help Grandad. Something's wrong with the solar panels; they aren't generating enough power.'

'What?' asked Sally? She stopped her berating of Brett. 'Is your house solar powered?'

'Yea,' said Jason worrying he had put his foot severely in his mouth. 'Isn't everyone's?'

'It's becoming a popular power source,' said Isabel in his ear. 'Some people are more serious about the environment than others. Your grandparents are extremely self-sufficient. Just don't tell them that the car runs on heated water and I think you're safe. Everything else is quite normal except the car engine rebuild – that's Micoron Hydrotechnology.'

'Great, thanks, Iz,' said Jason.

'What's great? Who's Iz?' asked Brett, turning to Jason and confronting him. 'Why are you always talking to yourself? The kids at school are calling you Casper as in he who talks to ghosts. I know, I know it doesn't quite work but they reckon you're always talking to someone and you have mentioned this Iz before.'

'Leave him alone, Brett. I talk to myself too, everyone does,' said Sally. 'That's fantastic about your house being solar powered – a real move in the right direction. We have solar water heating but we haven't even considered powering our whole house with solar yet. Well, I have, but Dad won't consider it now. It's a bit too costly until they build a good battery. Anyway, dinner. Are you coming? No, you said no. Okay, we will see you tomorrow.'

'But, I wanna know who this Iz is?'

'Come on,' said Sally dragging Brett by the hand down her street. 'I will let you help me cook.'

Jason continued down the road, waiting until they were completely out of sight before talking to Isabel again.

'Wow, that was close. What's a Casper? Is that bad? The whole school must think I am nuts,' he smiled to himself. 'Oh well, it could be worse. I could be talking to the Inkaba.' He shuddered. 'That wasn't funny. What made me think of that to compare this to? That would be dreadful.'

Chapter 8 – Dragon Healing

Sarah screamed. She was still whimpering when her dad arrived to pick her up. The school nurse stood over her, her expression worried. They had managed to coax Sarah out of class and into the sick bay, where she huddled on a bed.

'Honey, Saranah, what's wrong?' Walter asked stroking her hair and using her real name.

'Siiiaaann has been hurt. His wing is damaged. He might never fly again.'

'Who?' asked the nurse.

'Her... ummm … imaginary friend. Come on, sweetheart, let's go.'

With that Sarah passed out. Walter scooped her up in his arms.

In her dreams she went to Sian's side.

'Are you okay?' she whispered.

'It hurts,' replied Sian, a young blue dragon.

'Take him with you, Saranah,' said Martare in a deep voice. 'Take him to the waterfalls and distract him while we work on his wing. Zion has had trouble reaching him to take him there. We are glad you have come and he responds to you. He will be okay. He tore his wing badly when he appeared in front of a meteor. We think he was looking for Inkaba way out past the Sun Star. From what we can see from the pictures he shows us, his wing took the full impact. We are unsure of the details. We are having trouble seeing all that he saw and we don't know why he won't let us see everything. He seems to have blocked us so we have had trouble stopping the pain but we will discuss this when he is better.'

Sarah took Sian to the waterfalls in her mind. They were surrounded by a tall escarpment from which a strong current of green water cascaded down crashing loudly onto the black boulders below on which dragons often sunbaked. The waterfall was surrounded by trees with thick grey trunks covered in twisted vines with yellow and green leaves contrasting with the dark green and purple foliage of the trees. The ground nearest the water was sandy but light grey in colour. Among the trees were large red, purple and blue flowers half a metre in diameter growing wildly from the vines winding around the thick tree trunks. In her mind they settled on the grey sand to talk.

Diverting his attention, she told him about her day, and when that was done she started discussing her recent meeting with Jazz and what the latest update was on the Inkaba. She realised he probably already knew the news but could only keep him at the waterfall as long as she had his attention. Eventually she ran out of things to say so started singing him lullabies that her mother would have sung when she was a child. While she sang, she explored Sian's thoughts. She was able to block his pain while the older dragons worked on his wing.

Martare let a stray thought go, 'They might save it, but it would take much time.'

Eventually Sian drifted off to sleep on the warm sand, Sarah continuing to explore his thoughts, looking for the events of today. She agreed with Martare that there was something very wrong. Sian blocking his thoughts from her – he had never blocked her before. She could see and feel the impact, the ripping of tendons and the flapping of skin – a wing no longer able to be controlled. Then she could hear Zion's voice coaxing her, or Sian, back to Draco, showing the blue dragon directions and strong images of himself and where he sat, tensed, helping bring Sian home from the Sun Star.

'We have done all we can,' said Martare.

'His wing?' asked Sarah.

'Time will tell, dear one. It was very damaged. Zion clipped his own wings to provide more skin to work with: now its best they both sleep and recover. Did you find anything more?'

Zion, Sian's twin, had hatched from the same egg so it was even stranger that he could not reach his brother. Zion, more a blue-black than solid blue, was now double the size of Sian, so clipping his wings would have helped his brother. Although neither would be able to fly now for a couple of weeks. Dragon magic would speed healing enormously but could not completely erase time needed to heal.

'No, there is something blocking his thoughts. Maybe my visions will help. I had better go home now. If anything comes to me I will reach you.'

With that she woke. She was exhausted.

'Hummm ...'

A white fan cooling the room from above drew her attention.

'Sarah, you're okay,' said Dixie, running small vibrations through Sarah's necklace, where she carried her AI. It was Dixie's way of showing concern.

'Oh, Dixie, poor Sian,' she turned and sobbed into the pillow.

'Sarah,' said a voice from the doorway, 'how are you feeling, dear? You have been asleep for most of the day.'

Dixie must have told them she was awake. It was Frieda; her dad must have bought her to Josh and Frieda's.

'I'm okay. Is Whistle around? Can you ask him to talk to Martare, an elder from Draco? He will explain. I am really sleepy. Is it okay if I go back to sleep?'

'Of course, dear. You're in Jason's bed, so he might come in to grab some clothes, but otherwise he is quite comfortable on the fold-out couch in the lounge room, so don't worry about him.'

'Thankssss,' said Sarah falling back into a deep sleep.

She woke again later. The room was in darkness.

'Dixie, is there a small light in here? I'm hungry and need to get something to eat.'

A small lamp came on next to the bed. From the clock on the bedside table she could see it was after 1.00 am.

'Where's Dad?'

'Sleeping in the spare room. He and Josh spoke to Whistle and understand it is not a threat.' Dixie paused momentarily. 'Farah says your dad and Josh worked quite late and Frieda left you dinner in the fridge. We just need to zap it in the microwave. Do you know where you're going?'

With that the necklace illuminated to help Sarah see in the dark.

She was in the kitchen waiting for her food to heat up when Jason poked his head around the door.

'Hey, you feeling better?' asked Jason rubbing his eyes and leaning against the doorjamb. He had on a pair of stripy pyjama bottoms and his hair looked like someone had teased it.

'Sorry. I didn't mean to wake you.'

'You didn't. It's okay. Dixie told Isabel you had woken up and Isabel woke me to make sure you were okay.'

'Oh, thanks, Isabel. I am fine.'

'You're welcome. Dixie agrees; she has been monitoring your heart rate and vitals since you passed out. She says you are fine, especially now that you have slept soundly. The last sleep was a lot deeper,' noted Isabel.

'We understand from Whistle that you were able to go to the blue dragon and block his pain while Martare and the others worked on his damaged wing. That must have been pretty tiring,' said Jason.

Just then the microwave pinged, making them both jump.

'Come on. Let's sit at the kitchen table. I'm hungry too.'

He rifled around in the fridge extracting some milk and almond cookies. 'Do you want some milk too? Not sure how well it will go with that pasta. Maybe juice instead.'

'Milk will be fine, thank you.'

Quietly they munched their food, each involved in their own thoughts or half-asleep. Jason kept her company until she finished, finally placing the dishes in the sink and shooing her back in the direction of his room after she offered to take the couch.

'Go. I haven't been helping a dragon from light years away block out his pain. Go.' He smiled to soften the demand. 'It's rather chilly tonight. I am looking forward to getting back under that doona.' Tipping his head in the direction of the lounge room.

After the events of the day, Sarah went to sleep thinking of her premonition involving Jason. She smiled. It was becoming clearer that he would be able to save him, though she was still not sure how.

***

71

Josh and Walter stayed up late into the night talking about the day's events. They had had no idea Sarah's gifts were so strong. The ability to go telepathically to a dragon at will and help that dragon block pain when other dragons could not, sent their minds whirling. What did this mean? They had never heard of such a relationship with dragons before. Dragons and seers had been known to pass messages between planets. But how had she known the blue was in trouble? How had she known to go to him? Had she just been waiting for Walter to arrive before she went to him? Could she have gone sooner if she wanted? The questions were endless. They had to talk to Sarah. Frieda had stopped them before they convinced themselves that it was okay to wake her up. They had known it wasn't but struggled to keep themselves from knocking on her door. They had to talk to Sarah and then Faroon. What else could Sarah do? Could she help find the Inkaba if she looked?

***

The day dragged on. Jason had been looking forward to this game all week. Most of the school was coming down to watch them beat the Titans. Sarah had been asleep when he left in the morning with Josh and Walter waiting expectantly for her to rise.

'*Brriiinngg* ...' The 2.30 pm bell finally rang.

'Yeah, wohoo,' the class cheered.

'So, Jason,' asked Julia from the dance committee, 'are you going to win? I heard the last couple of times the Titans have won but this time we might have a chance with you in the team. Is that true?'

'Yeah, we have a good team.'

'Great! Well, I'll be cheering for you then,' said Julia, smiling shyly before walking off.

'Oh, no,' said Brad coming up behind Jason and resting his hands on his shoulders.

'What's oh no?' Jason responded.

'I think she likes you,' replied Jamie shaking his head with a goofy grin.

'Come on, Romeo,' said Brett. 'You sure do attract them.'

'I've got to head to the lockers to get changed. I'll see you guys at the game.' He picked up his books, put them in his backpack and swung it over his shoulder while trying not to look annoyed.

Once the guys were out of earshot, he spoke to Isabel.

'Who's this Romeo then? That's the second time I have been called Romeo. I tell you this planet is obsessed with names. As if it isn't hard enough to remember my name is currently Jason, I now apparently go by Casper and Romeo, too.'

Isabel let out a chuckle, again making her seem more human than machine.

'Romeo was in love with Juliet. Central characters in a romantic tragedy written by William Shakespeare – it does not end well. However, these days, Romeo is sometimes a name given to those who are popular with the opposite sex. It might be a compliment.'

'What? When have I ever been successful with the opposite sex? These humans are whacked. They rarely make sense.'

'I think it's just to be taken in jest.'

'Jest! I'm not sure I find it funny, Isabel,' Jason fumed going red with embarrassment and anger simultaneously. At least he finally understood the term.

***

All jeering was forgotten by the time he reached the change room and found the team already there. Time to suit up and rally their energy for the contest. They were all wearing singlets and knee-length shorts in team colours of blue and gold. He watched as one team member streaked blue paint across the faces of other players. Isabel informed him it was something people did before going into battle, so Jason assumed this was a metaphor for how they planned to play – but then again who knew with these crazy Earthlings? Maybe they just liked to dress up. Isabel had laughed at that too as Jason muttered it under his breath. Remembering he wasn't completely alone on this crazy planet, he relaxed a bit. He would always have Isabel.

The Jaguars entered the auditorium.

'Hurrah. Yay Jaguars. Wahoo – go team!' the crowd cheered.

A sea of blue and gold streamers covered the bleachers, various songs could be heard. Words of encouragement for the Jaguars, something about maiming and wiping the floor with the Titans – slightly aggressive – although Jason thought the tune was catchy.

Crowds of students from Jacobs High filled the bleachers – the auditorium was packed.

'*Tweet.*' The whistle blew.

The Titans wore red and black. Jason only had a couple of centimetres on his opponent. A relief to have someone almost at eye level for a change. At the first ball toss, his opponent jumped higher, flicking the ball to one of his teammates who, with no effort at all, managed to make his way towards the goal for an easy lay-up. The crowd booed, all except a small pocket of cheering red and black supporters.

The Jaguars rallied. After this initial setback, training kicked in. Just before half-time, the teams were neck and neck. Suddenly a Titan, a rather tall dark-haired lad, blocked a lay-up from Jason but, for moving his feet, the referee called, 'Foul. That's a penalty shot, son. Your ball yellow.' He tossed the ball to Jason.

The teams crowded around, the spectators suddenly hushing.

'So, you going to be able to make the shot, Princess?' It was the same Titan that had caused the foul. The small crowd of supporters the Titans had brought with them roared with laughter as did the rest of the Titans. The referee gave the boy a stern look.

For the second time that day, Jason blushed a deep red. The Titans laughed harder. Their supporters started pointing and chanting, 'Princess, Princess, Princess.'

Jason was mad.

'Oh, that's it ... Princess? Is that the best you can come up with? Do you really think calling me Princess is going to offend me so much that I will forget how to aim for that metal circle thing? What a genius plan,' yelled Jason, looking hard at the boy who had suddenly gone quiet. And with that, while still looking at the boy, Jason made the shot one handed.

'You made it,' whispered Isabel in his ear just before the crowd roared and the half-time whistle blew.

Jason breathed out, heavily. He hadn't realised he had been holding his breath. There had been a fair bit of luck but it was also a move Jason had played on Micoron. He just practised certain shots again and again, ensuring his feet were on the right spot on the line, then closed his eyes and just went through the same motions. He had practised the same thing with the basketball after school while waiting for training to start.

While the crowd was settling, the coach, his face very red, pulled Jason aside. He looked hot.

'That was a lucky shot, son; it could have gone both ways. Next time can you try looking at where you are shooting? We would like to beat this team.' He half-grinned, pushing Jason on the back towards the bench. A couple of students were passing out water.

And they did beat the Titans 87 to 84 with Jason shooting at least half the points for the game. The crowd was ecstatic. Julia had come running up to him after the game and thrown her arms around his neck. Not sure what to do, he had prised her off his neck and set her down nicely to the side while the crowd continued to pat the team, Jason especially, on the back by way of congratulations.

'Kai finished ten minutes ago; they won by two points.' said Sally reading off her mobile.

The girl's team had played their game over at the Titans' home ground.

'Looks like Jacobs are winners all round.'

Chapter 9 – Ultimate Weapon

One of the lead ships had come upon a blue. Their position almost uncovered. Captain Trane, reading the report off the screen, frowned. The blue just appeared in front of the ship, his lead ship, its back to the vessel. It must have been scouting sporadically, appearing then disappearing, then reappearing next to stars or planets seen as specks in the distance. Luckily the captain of the ship had thought fast, ejecting one of the waste disposal units straight at the blue. The blue had been injured. In shock long enough for the ship's physician, Master Ezann, to enter and bind its mind. The hope was to have the dragon expel the air in its lungs, causing death. However, the dragon had vanished. The physician struggled to maintain the bind on the blue. Binding, especially the mind of a dragon, had rendered Master Ezann and his two assistants useless. All their available energy locked up in controlling the dragon's thoughts – or lack thereof. Between them they decided to slowly delete the recent memories of the blue, ensuring their position would not be recalled.

They worked to block all from entering the mind of the blue to aid him. Their fear, that someone would see the moments leading up to his injuries. The dragon had not seen them, luckily, but another might come to investigate if they could get a good position on the attack location. This would lead them to the Inkabas travelling past the sun towards their new home. The crew were currently making adjustments to their drive. It would be a few more hours before they could make the required large jumps across the galaxy.

The captain was furious. How had these dragons become involved in this pursuit? How had they known that the Inkaba were travelling? There must be a leak within his lines, one that he must find. He ordered his ship's physicians to link minds with the physicians aboard the lead ship. They could not allow the blue to recover – too much at stake. His whole race could potentially perish if they did not move soon.

At Captain Trane's command, his physicians went to their quarters to meditate. They would provide energy for Master Ezann and his cronies from the lead ship. They would link minds with the physician as commanded, but one, Master Olingy, would not necessarily aid him. He had other ideas, ones that better suited his plans. Luckily, he was the stronger physician so he had a slim chance of actually pulling off this little change of plan.

***

Friday arrived. Jason had school all day before heading to the gym to decorate it for the dance. Because of last night's basketball game, they now had only a few hours to hang the flower garlands from the ceiling, set up the small sandpit and deck chairs they had planned for the corner of the gym, plus add all the little touches needed to make the gym tropical, including showing the tree hire people how to create the palm-lined entry.

They had picked up outfits during the week from the local op shop. Gaudy Hawaiian inspired shirts and board shorts. They had also raided Frieda's garden for frangipani flowers, placing them in the fridge to stop them wilting. His grandmother had promised to drive these down to the gym at the last minute. Packing his clothes for the evening, he threw in his rubber thongs, before heading off to school.

***

Master Ezann had just come across something unusual. While going through the blue's memories, he had reached up to scratch his own ear. To his surprise the dragon had also raised his claw and scratched his head. With the energy supplied by the other physicians, eight in total, Master Ezann had been able to work faster, removing the sequence of events that had led the blue to their location. Maybe it was providing him with more control than he first thought. He tried it again. This time he clapped his hands together, then rubbed them. It worked. The blue followed. However, this time it had been harder. It was as if the blue had expected it and tried to resist. The paws had not quite met in the middle and the rubbing had kind of been in the air, but Master Ezann had still controlled it.

Ezann and the other physicians had placed the dragon in a deep sleep while they remained linked with the blue. It was the only way they could keep the other dragons from entering his mind. If they were able to get inside the blue's mind, the Inkaba physicians would be found out for sure.

He turned to one of his seconds, Anush. 'Did you see that, Anush? I must teleport to the other ship and inform Trane. Take over. Do not fiddle,' he said, with a stern stare at his apprentice. Master Ezann had been drawing power only from the other physicians but now Anush looked directly into the mind of the dragon where previously he had just been providing support.

With Master Ezann out of the way, Olingy went to work. 'Sian,' he sang. 'Sian,' he sang again. The Inkaba could not hear song; music was like a foreign language to them, burblings or constant noise, but not song.

'Sian, it is Olingy. I am here. Can you hear me? You must be strong; you must break this magic. You are strong, blue dragon.'

In the distance, very quietly, he heard a response.

'Too sleepy, Olin. Makes me slee ... pee.'

'Sian, Sian,' he sung again.

'Shhhhhh, I am sleeping,' came the gruff reply.

Something had happened that Anush could not understand. An eerie humming that had disappeared almost as soon as it had started. Still, he had been told not to fiddle, so did not go looking for the source of the humming but instead continued removing each frame of the memories leading up to the blue's accident. It was tedious work and Anush was lazy – albeit very clever at hiding his laziness. If he just removed snips of memory here and there, the blue couldn't possibly piece the events together again – nor could anyone else for that matter.

Anush spent the next hour randomly snipping at the blue's memories. The other wizards continued to aid his strength as he worked on the blue. They did not see what he saw. Carelessly, Anush didn't notice when he started snipping away, not just at the recent event but at Sian's memories of himself as a young dragon and of his twin brother. Only when Anush fell asleep did the hacking stop and Olingy's consciousness came back trying to raise Sian's awareness again. This time he was horrified to see what had been done to the blue. He must think. He disconnected his support so that Anush could no longer benefit from any of his strength and made his way over to his bed. Rest might help clear his mind, but rest did not come to the physician despairing over the fate of the young blue and wondering what could possibly be done to aid him. He wanted to contact other dragons or his fellow Micoronians but he knew that to do so would jeopardise the whole mission and the years he had spent embedded with the Inkaba. He must find a way to save the beautiful blue dragon – his friend.

***

As usual, when waiting for an event to commence, the day dragged. There was a lot of talk of Jason's amazing goal and many a pat on the back from guys or winks from girls. The girl winks always ended with them turning back to their friends and giggling while stealing looks at Jason. Jason had no date for the dance. Some of the students had paired up but between basketball, the dance planning and school, none of Jason's crew had quite got around to it; not that it mattered. Kai had also convinced her parents to let her go, so at least there was a mixed group, if anyone wanted to dance – not that the boys would be dancing. Apparently, it was frowned upon here on Earth. Again, Jason was confused. Being rather athletic, he was naturally a great dancer, where he came from anyway, and Micoronians loved to dance. But if dancing at a school dance wasn't cool then he would stick to drinks duty and whatever else these Earthlings did at a dance with no dancing.

'Very confusing race these Earthlings,' Jason mentioned to Isabel on his way to the hall to decorate. The schoolwork and study wasn't the hard part; it was the randomness of cultural behaviour and social norms that really confused him. For a start, boys and girls were considered equal, yet guys were still expected to lift all the heavy stuff and carry anything dirty while holding open doors at the same time. He had learnt this very quickly from being on the dance committee. The girls had taken to ordering the guys around and asking for help to move even the lightest object. He also got a very serious serve when he didn't use his foot to hold the door open for one of the girls even though he was carrying a box probably three times as heavy as the empty esky being carried by the girl.

'Wow, Isabel, I can't believe we have been here so long already. I wonder what the guys back home are doing,' said Jason just as they reached the hall doors.

'Probably getting ready for a game of Battle Bowl and afterwards, a real dance,' said Isabel matter-of-factly.

Jason had known the typical Friday night plans. His question had been more whimsical rather than really seeking information but Iz's answer set his gut clenching – homesickness overwhelmed him.

'Sure, would be nice to hang out with some "normal" fellow Micoronians,' he managed after some time. 'Oh well. Come on, Isabel. I guess we should go and get ready for this dance. I think we still have a few decorations to sort.'

Isabel played some Micoronian music while Jason worked. It was a fast-tracked song cut through with instrumental rips. It helped him power through setting up chairs, lecterns and microphones but it hampered his ability to hear Brett and Sally yelling at him to get his attention. It was only when Isabel noted their calls and cut the music that he focused on the others. He had been putting out chairs and had inadvertently started to dance along with the beat, so much so that the others had stopped work to watch him. Especially after he had run up the wall and flipped backwards off it; that had definitely got everyone's attention.

'Don't tell me you can dance too,' said Brett. 'Bloody hell, mate. Can you leave some things for the rest of us to be good at? Jeez!' said Brett storming off to help set up lights with Allan.

'Wow!' said Clarissa.

'That was great,' said Sally, 'and I thought Brett and his brother were good dancers. Not that they would ever dance tonight but I know they can both dance. Remember, Angela, in Year 7 that routine they both did for assembly? Similar to what you did, Jason, but they could only stand on one hand or spin on their head. I don't think they can flip like that.'

'Hey, Brett,' yelled Angela. 'Can you flip or just spin on your head.'

'Great. Thanks, mate. Again, really appreciate it.' yelled back Brett. 'Just,' he said, accentuating the J, 'spin on my head. That used to be a pretty cool move.' Jason shrugged, embarrassed at having being caught out. Luckily, no-one mentioned that he had been dancing to no music – well, none that they could hear.

'Hey,' said Jason to change the subject and cover any more dancing disasters he might have, 'how about we get some tunes going? Allan, can you get that sound system your dad lent us working?'

A couple of hours before the dance started, the room looked great. Good as any auditorium could look dressed like a beach. Deck chairs in sand sat in one corner. Punch bowls surrounded by palm trees in another. Frangipanis floating in bowls of water on randomly placed tables and Hawaiian music planned for later. Hanging from the roof and basketball rings were long garlands of fake flowers. On the stage, behind the lectern, a painted canvas of a rather large wave swung from the ceiling – compliments of the art department. They were all set. Everything ready for the students to arrive.

***

'Hey guys, this is fantastic. I can't believe how much work you did,' said Kai coming up behind the twins. By now the auditorium was filling with students.

'He didn't help,' replied Brad shoving Brett.

'As if,' replied Brett shoving his brother back. 'Sally, Jason and I did this with the rest of the committee. Brad couldn't work if his life depended on it.'

'Oh well, he's got me there. Save me a dance, Kai, I have to go meet Jamie out front. His mum was dropping him off after his dentist appointment,' said Brad wandering off.

'Oh, fine,' replied Kai shyly.

'Actually, you should save a dance for Jason, Kai,' said Sally coming up behind the group with Jason. 'This boy can really move.'

Rolling his eyes, Brett shoved Jason playfully

'At least he can't fight as good as me,' said Brett, throwing a mock punch at Jason and dancing back and forth on his feet at the same time. Jason ignored the swings from his mate. He didn't want to reveal to Brett that he was trained in a number of forms of combat. Micoronians trained in combat, not to fight, only for defence. Jason didn't need his friend to know he excelled in another area.

'Well, we should definitely dance later, Jason, and Brad too, of course,' said Sally. 'Did you come with someone, Kai, or do you want to hang out with us tonight? Unfortunately, we all have various jobs during the night but we're not all doing them at once,' noted Sally.

'Sounds great,' replied Kai. 'I would love to.'

The evening went very well. Brad came and claimed his dance with Kai. It was a slow number and although they were a bit awkward, they seemed to work it out eventually. Brett, Sally, Jamie and Jason all exchanged glances.

'I didn't know Brad liked Kai,' said Sally to Jamie.

'Me neither. But now that you mention it, he has talked about her a couple of times since the fete, but I hadn't thought anything of it,' responded Jamie.

'Her dad's not going to like that,' said Brett, 'even if he is my brother. You and Brad have got terrible reputations around here,' he said to Jamie.

After the dance, Kai and Brad disappeared into the crowd and then reappeared a little later near the drinks stand where Jason and Sally had been selling punch and soft drinks. Luckily, each time Julia had come up to ask Jason for a dance he had been busy filling cups with punch or helping Allan pick music and then, when he was free, Julia was filling cups or undertaking 'committee duties'. It wasn't that he disliked Julia but was not a fan of the way she bullied people to get her own way.

'Where have you been?' asked Brett accusingly of his brother. Kai blushed and Jason elbowed Brett in the ribs.

'Oh, really? No,' said Brett looking from Kai to Brad. 'You like him?' he said pointing at Brad and looking at Kai.

Brett went to walk off before pausing and adding, 'I mean, your taste in looks is exceptional, but your taste in brothers needs more work.'

Jamie snorted at that, shooting punch out his nose. This caused everyone to laugh, even Kai, as Brad snuck his hand into hers giving it a squeeze. Brett tried to keep a straight face but ended up joining in the laughter with his friends.

After the dance ended, Frieda and the twins' mum were waiting outside to ferry all the students home. Kai's parents were picking her up separately so they all said their goodbyes inside. They didn't want Kai's parents to see her hanging out with the troublesome two.

***

They had raised enough money from their fundraising activities so that each student only needed to pay a couple of hundred each to attend the camp. Clarissa's dad owned a few service stations in town and had made a reasonable donation to help the students get on their way and allowed them to set up a car wash in his petrol station for a couple of weekends. His customers had been so impressed by how polite the students were and so complimentary about their work that her dad had rung the principal and told him he would like to reward their good behaviour by lending them a couple of touring buses he had bought to convert into motor homes. Removing bus rental had saved heaps, and since a couple of teachers had licences suitable for driving buses, that brought the students costs down even further.

It was now a waiting game. Three weeks to kill before the big camp. They kept busy with basketball, ate at each other's houses and even went to the movies again. Kai had been allowed to come to most events, even dinner at Jason's house, as Kai's dad had been in Singapore on business for a bit and her mum was more lenient in regard to her daughter's activities. Her mum had even stayed to have dinner with Frieda and the twins' mum one night while Jason, Sally, Kai, Brett, Brad and Jamie cooked dinner outside on the BBQ.

It was during a trip to the movies that everything went wrong. Brad and Kai had walked out of the movie hand in hand and Kai's dad, instead of waiting in the car as usual, had come inside to collect Kai and seen them holding hands. Kai had dropped Brad's hand and walked quickly to the car with her father not far behind.

The next day before school, they found Kai sitting at one of the tables in the quad under a big tree – their usual haunt. Her eyes were puffy and red. Brad immediately sat down and grabbed her hand.

'What happened?' he asked as everyone plonked down around Kai. 'You can't see me anymore, can you?'

Kai shook her head. 'And,' she whispered, 'I can't go to camp. Mum tried to reason with him but there was no hope. My parents still aren't talking to each other and Dad was gone before I got up this morning. I am in real trouble. I can't remember the last time I was actually in real trouble.'

'What? You can't go to camp?' Jamie spoke first.

'That's terrible,' said Sally, sitting down and grabbing Kai's other hand.

'Well, I am not going either then,' said Brad firmly. He'd changed since meeting Kai. Even securing a B in one of his classes and, without Brad and Jamie leading each other astray, Jamie had also got an A in home economics when his soufflé was the only one to rise.

'Don't be silly, Brad,' said Kai managing a smile. 'It's only a week and I still have classes I can attend. What will you do for the week? I was only going because I got sick when my French class went for their school trip to France and Sally's dad just tried to make up for it. Out of your classes, there is hardly anyone not going to the Alice and those students are just going to the library to study between some regular classes. It will be terribly boring for you to stay.'

'I'll think about it. What you're saying does make some sense,' said Brad, not sounding convinced.

***

'So, what you're saying,' said Captain Trane, 'is that you think you can control the dragon's actions. This could be useful. Quick get back to your ship before that idiot does something to the blue and let me think about how we can use this to our advantage. Keep working on controlling the blue. It would be good of course if you had no resistance.'

Ezann bowed and left but didn't return immediately to the lead ship. Instead, he made a quick detour to the ship's library to download any literature he could find on dragons that might help him better understand and control the blue.

Chapter 10 – The Big Camp

Finally, the day came for them all to leave for camp. Everyone, including the teachers, was excited.

Whistle's last-minute instructions from the night before on how to contact him were fresh in Jason's mind. Isabel would contact Dixie who would get Sarah to call Whistle. Easy. Everyone was still reeling from learning about Sarah's ability to speak to dragons at will and what it could mean. Unfortunately, although she could tell that Sian was well, she could no longer speak to him. She shared with the Keepers that Master Olin had appeared to her when she was reaching for Sian too. But he was gone before she could call to him. This had added an extremely puzzling aspect to the saga of the blue, albeit a happy one. It was good for all to know that Olin lived – somewhere. Especially as Sarah had advised he was well.

Frieda had helped Jason pack. While Whistle, sitting on Jason's bed, had given the instructions on how he could be contacted.

Board shorts for swimming were packed for use in waterfalls on the way down. A thick sweater and jeans as it actually got quite cold in Alice Springs of an evening. Sneakers for trekking, a beach towel, toiletries and a few other items of relevance including a digital camera and some scissors for his hair. Isabel had a brilliant recording system that would take better photos than any human camera but asking his friends to smile while he held up his ring would have them thinking he was strange again. Isabel was also able to emit a low frequency field that would keep the bugs away from Jason, so really other than sunscreen for his fair skin and a few clothes, all he needed to add was a hat and plenty of socks and jocks.

Everyone gathered in front of the school at 7.30 am. Alice Springs could be reached in less than a day but the group had plans to make a few stops on the way down. Teachers were keen for an early start in order to be gone before students who were not going on the camp started arriving for school – less confusion that way.

With bags packed and stowed under the three large coaches and the roll called, it was time to go.

'*Beep beep.*' Brad's phone alerted him to a message.

```
Have a wonderful trip and I want loads of photos and
stories when you get back xx Kai
```

```
We promise. See you soon xx Brad, Sal, Jas, Brett, J
```

Jamie and Brad jumped on first, saving the whole back seat for Sally, Jason and Brett. Mr Wright read out the rules around expected student behaviour. Obviously picking up on the excitement from the students, he smiled the whole time as he read out a list of dos and dont's for the trip, including calling parents if any rules were broken.

First planned stop, Litchfield. A place of many waterfalls and rock pools. Next stop, Katherine for the night. From Katherine to Tennant Creek, and then Alice Springs for a night. Uluru, then Kings Canyon and back to Alice Springs before driving straight up to Darwin. All in all, just over seven days of touring.

Ms Johnson was reading through the list of all the activities they had brought on the journey to keep the students entertained – DVDs, travel Scrabble and chess, crosswords, Sudoku and a mix of books and comics.

Jason and Sally grabbed the chess set as it was passed around. Brad, Jamie and Brett opted for comics.

Having left the main road and passed through the town of Bachelor, they were heading down a rather windy road surrounded by hills and bush taking them into Litchfield National Park.

'First stop is Tolmer Falls,' Ms Johnson announced.

Only a short hike from the carpark to the falls. Many students ran from the bus to the viewing platform, claiming, 'First.'

'Isabel, look. Isn't it gorgeous? It's so like Draco. All it needs is another moon above and we could be there.'

'Agreed,' said Isabel, using her improved access to see.

'Where's Draco?' asked Jamie. 'Brad told me you talk to yourself. Who is this Isabel?'

'He's not talking to Isabel, again is he?' asked Sally finally too curious not to comment.

'Who is she then?' asked Brad 'An old girlfriend or something?'

'An imaginary friend?' asked Brett seriously.

Turning redder, Jason shrugged. For a second, it flashed through his head to tell his friends the truth, but before he could give it any serious consideration they were summoned back to the bus. After a couple of extra strange long looks from Sally and Brad, they all started back up the small incline towards their buses.

A hot day. The next stop would allow them time to cool off with a swim. Those around Jason were trying to convince him there were crocodiles in the water. Isabel, correcting their jokes, assured him there were not likely to be any man-eaters. Possibly a few freshwater crocs but they tended to keep out of everyone's way.

'But avoid standing on them,' she suggested.

The day was passing quickly. After swimming at a couple of different waterfalls, they enjoyed an early lunch of BBQ sausages, onions, bread and sauce under some shady trees. It was now early afternoon and they were hitting the road again. They needed to make it to Katherine well before dusk. Driving on the roads at nightfall was dangerous. Loads of wildlife crossing the road or lying on it to absorb the last of the day's heat. Driving at night was also against school policy, given the risks.

The drive from Litchfield to Katherine was much further than the run down from Darwin. So, after a brief period, most students quietened down, subdued by their earlier exertions hiking and swimming. Sally drifted off against the window, her head on her jumper. Brad, Brett and Jamie had pulled out iPods and were listening to each other's music. Jason declined the offer of shared earphones preferring to immerse himself in travel books and maps of Alice Springs, Uluru and Kings Canyon. He was amazed to find that Uluru was only the tip of the great rock. Most of it lay hidden under the ground.

Reaching Katherine just after 4.00 pm, they passed two rows of strip shops on either side of the main road that made up the city centre. Continuing along the Stuart Highway took them out the other side – streets dissecting the main road as they drove past. Their destination was an old scout hall, their camp for the night. They would eat in the main hall that was surrounded by many small cabins each sleeping four people. The boys would all sleep together in the same cabin. Sally went off to find her roommates soon after they had pulled up and reclaimed their bags.

Jason, entering the cabin – or as Jamie referred to it 'the donga' – found himself shoved aside as Jamie and Brad raced past him, laying claim to the two top bunks. Brett and Jason had to settle for the lower two. Rolling out sleeping bags over the mattresses, they placed their pillows at the head of their beds.

'Should we go for a kick?' asked Jamie.

Luckily, Jason had watched the boys at school kick the footy around and had purchased one with his pocket money. He had practised kicking the strange oval red leather ball around his grandparents' property in case he ever got the chance to play. It had been Isabel's idea. She was always Googling, absorbing the literature on the latest trends and fads for young people as well as other items of interest to both herself and Jason.

What started with four soon grew to ten with students taking turns to take a 'mark'. Some girls had plonked down nearby to watch while chatting amongst themselves. It was mostly boys playing but Sally had joined in, holding her own, kicking further than some of the boys and gaining her fair share of marks along with another girl, Jennifer, who Jason couldn't remember seeing around before.

After playing hard for an hour they were interrupted by Ms Stokes calling out it was time to start dinner. The teachers had grouped the students into work teams. Assigning each team tasks to help prepare, cook and clean up after dinner. None of the boys were teamed together. Sally was also in a different work group. This progressed their jobs as there were fewer distractions. Jason figured this was an intentional move by the teachers. Jamie's group was making salads, Sally's was BBQ-ing, Brett's, setting tables, while Brad buttered a pile of bread rolls. Jason, who was on clean-up duty later, relaxed watching a small television in the corner of the hall with the other students on clean-up duties.

'We're going to have think about your hair soon, Jason,' said Isabel after they had finished dinner that night. Jason was taking out the trash to the bins located out the back of the hall.

'Agreed. Any suggestions?'

'Probably none that you're going to like. The only thing I can think of is a middle of the night wake-up call. But that's still risky if someone were to walk in on you. Or, we can leave it a day or two between cuts. I mean people seeing you every day might not notice it growing so quickly. We have gone a day or two before.'

'Yeah, we could cut it in a cubicle, but I think a mirror would come in handy.'

Reaching for the bin lid, he recoiled suddenly when a clawed hand lifted the lid.

'Whistle!' exclaimed Jason, pleased to see his scaly mate. 'What are you doing here? Is everything okay? Have you got any news?' Jason continued becoming more concerned, a frown deepening across his brow.

'Was listening to you and Izzy. I may have a solution for you. Are you done here? Where are your scissors?'

'In my bag. Why?'

Vanishing. Reappearing moments later wiggling scissors in front of Jason. Grabbing Jason's hand, they both vanished, reappearing in Jason's bathroom.

'No-one here,' said Whistle. 'Sorry you can't say hello to your grandparents. At least you can cut your hair in peace. Try being quick though so no-one misses you. I am going to look in your fridge. Whistle hungry.'

'You're a star, Whistle.'

Returning to camp ten minutes later, neatly trimmed, Jason passed the evening with the others singing around the campfire, toasting marshmallows. Mr Wright strummed a guitar while the students tried to remember the words to popular Australian songs.

***

Captain Trane smiled. Surely it wasn't going to be that simple. The power of a dragon at his disposal during this invasion. Couldn't be possible, he argued with himself – far too easy. Turning to his servant, his brow furrowing, he snarled, 'Find Olingy for me. We must talk. We cannot allow Ezann to mess this one up.' He was speaking more to himself than his servant who had already rushed off to fulfil his order.

Moments later.

'Master Olingy,' said Captain Trane. He was seated at a large black table, his back to the magician, gazing out a large window. There was little to see, just blackness dotted with pinpricks of light – deep space. He clasped his arms across his broad chest. He was wearing a tight black suit under his silver war armour, arms bulging, straining against the black material.

'Master,' responded Olingy, practised at keeping the tone of disgust out of his voice and off his face. He waited for the Captain to continue.

'You're linked with Ezann. You saw the blue he works with. We have good news. It seems, by some miracle, the blue responds to Ezann's will. We may have the best attack mechanism available to us to ensure victory in our upcoming war.'

'Master,' replied Olingy, shocked. 'What do you mean, responds to his will?'

Trane laughed. 'I am told,' he laughed again, a horrible deep laugh that had no mirth in it. 'I am told,' he repeated, 'that Ezann can make the dragon move and act as he likes. Maybe ...' he stopped, turning from the window, 'with practice, and your help, we could use the dragon to aid us in our endeavours.'

This time Olin struggled hard to keep the look of disgust off his face. Trane, misunderstanding his look, grew serious. 'You will work with Ezann, Olingy. This is important to our race. I care nothing for your personal dislike of Ezann. I have no patience for your emotion, it is nothing. Go. Go now, and work with Ezann. Go to his ship and offer your *full* will. We have a good chance of a quick battle now. I will not accept failure. If we fail it will be your head and Ezann's too,' he said turning back to the window. 'Get out!' This yelled with such force Olingy almost ran from the room.

Shaking with fear either for what had just happened, what he had heard, what might happen to him next or for the young blue – he was not sure. Maybe it was all of these. He did not stop running until he was back in his office. Closing the door, he leant heavily against it. Air was shuddering in and out of his chest, his mind whirling with fear and possibilities.

'Oh, Sian,' he whispered quietly, 'what can I do?' He must get help, but how? He needed to think but had no time. If only he could talk to the Keepers, or Josh – Josh would have some ideas. He thought of his old friend a moment, a friend he had not seen for many years, not since the invasion of Sarth. After the invasion he had been sent, posing as a renegade magician, a criminal fleeing his planet, to seek refuge with the enemy. This ruse had not been easy. Years of working tirelessly as a servant to the Inkaba – in reality their slave – until one day his knowledge stopped a virus sweeping through their villages. He had prevented it killing their offspring. Saving many Inkaba young redeemed his status as a trusted ally. Trane kept him close so he could not stray. He was afforded the luxury of being counted as one of the many healing magicians that served the Inkaba – tending to their wounded, caring for their young.

He had no friends, only the dragons. They came to him in his mind, keeping him sane, alleviating loneliness. But since the Inkaba set out on this mission, he had been unable to communicate with them. It was far too dangerous with so many physicians on board. Trying to contact anyone could easily expose him. Sian and his brother had often kept Olin company during his time with the Inkaba. There had been one other keeping watch on the Inkaba, but she had remained behind on Sarth with the other women. She was of Inkaba descent, but had been raised by the Pedite race, having been left behind after a battle long ago. She had offered to go back to the Inkaba as she wanted to understand her culture. She did not know about Olin and he had not heard much about her since her infiltration. He knew not if her loyalties still lay with the Keepers or if she had come to believe in everything her culture could teach her.

Pondering all this, thoughts swirling around his head, he sifted through his knowledge, experience and relationships to find a solution to what was coming. If only he knew the Inkaba's destination, then maybe he could risk a communication with the outside to warn the Keepers about Sian and about the impending invasion. It could mean his death, but what other options did he have?

***

Whistle and Jason made arrangements to meet up every second night so that Whistle could update Jason and help him cut his hair without getting himself caught. In reality, Isabel could keep him updated so Jason secretly thought Whistle's visits were to give his grandfather – or his grandmother – an opportunity to keep an eye on him. He wasn't quite sure who had suggested the thought to Whistle. It certainly made things easier with his hair and Jason quite enjoyed the dragon's company. It also gave him an opportunity to get away and chat to Isabel. With everyone sleeping in the same room, eating together and using the refreshing rooms at the same time, it left little time for chatting to his AI. Jason was not the only one finding this frustrating. Isabel had also raised her concerns that they had never gone this long without talking. They had cut down when he had started at the Earth school but still, they could talk mornings and afternoons. Here they could barely say good morning without feeling like they were going to get caught. Jason had taken to tapping with his nail to answer Isabel's questions. Once for yes, twice for no, but this was extremely limiting. By the time Whistle came to get him the night they arrived in Alice Springs, he was busting to get out a half-decent conversation with his best friend. In addition to hearing her take on everything they had seen and done over the last couple of days.

Whistle came to get him from the room where they were sleeping in Tennant Creek as soon as he was sure the other boys were asleep. He didn't speak, just appeared, then, touching Jason's hand, he catapulted them across the country back to Jason's home, appearing in the lounge room where Frieda was watching the television with Porus.

'Jason!' exclaimed Frieda. 'Whistle, what on earth are you two up to?'

Whistle, smiling his usual goofy grin, simply said, 'Haircut time.'

'Of course, aren't you two clever? But it's so late, Jason. Shouldn't you be asleep?'

'I am, I mean was,' he replied yawning. 'I was expecting you most of the night,' he said turning to Whistle, 'but I couldn't seem to get a moment alone.'

'I have watched,' replied Whistle. 'This was the first opportunity I had to grab you. Must friends go with you everywhere?'

'Apparently,' replied Jason. 'Isabel. How are you? Gee, this is terrible. How did we not think of some better way to communicate before we left on this excursion? I haven't spoken to you in days. How am I going to last for another week? Gran, this is torture. Can you come and get me?'

Freida smiled. 'This is good practice for the two of you. Jason has more years at school here, and you'll work something out. If you're hungry, Whistle, there are some defrosted steaks in the fridge. Everything is frozen in threes but with Jason away there is no-one here to eat his share and Josh doesn't need an extra steak.'

Whistle waddled off towards the kitchen. Jason wandered down the hall to the bathroom to start on his hair. They didn't stay long, just long enough for Whistle to finish his steak and Jason to cut his hair. Whistle had to get back to some of the younger Z-dragons who had recently arrived from Draco to take over from those who had been scouting for the last few months.

Chapter 11 – Time to Explain

Today saw three opportunities on offer.

There was so much to do in Alice Springs that, with three buses available, students had three choices for the day. In the morning they could visit the desert park, ride a camel or go on a tour of Alice and surrounds. They would all meet up for lunch and, in the afternoon, they could choose another of the three activities missing out on only one option for the day.

Should the friends all stick together for the morning or not? After much debate, it was decided that they would all visit the Alice Springs Desert Park together but in the afternoon Sally and Jason would go on the tour of the Alice and surrounds, while the others would take a camel ride down the dry bed of the Finke River.

'How cool is this place?' spruiked Jamie.

Set in the red dirt of central Australia, the Desert Park was home to loads of local flora and fauna. Because there were lizards involved, Whistle decided to tag along incognito. It was funny for Jason to see the occasional footprint or tail swirl appear in the soil near the group as Whistle landed to explore something in more detail or to wait for the group.

'What are you smiling at?' asked Sally. So funny to watch that Jason was hanging out to tell someone but decided instead to point out a large bird with beady eyes, eyeing them from a distance.

'I think he thinks either we are his lunch or have his lunch.' Sally nodded in agreement, tucking the popcorn that she had brought to feed to a few select animals back in her pocket for safekeeping.

In the afternoon they visited Anzac Hill, local art galleries, an old telegraph station and the School of the Air where students from outback cattle stations conducted their schoolwork over radios and computers. They purchased souvenirs from Alice Springs mall before stopping briefly at a small wildlife park that housed a very large crocodile and some smaller lizards and snakes. Again,

Whistle's presence was notable as the dragon, on seeing the gigantic crocodile swimming in a pool at the back of the small park, blew out a little puff of fire.

That evening they joined the rest of their group around outdoor BBQs. Tonight's accommodation was at a local caravan park. The boys once again teamed up to share a four-bed cabin. Again, there were bunk beds but Jason happily settled for the bottom bunk.

He was sitting on a wooden park bench next to the fire, just finishing his sausage and salad when Isabel spoke in his ear, 'Jason, you have to go back to the cabin. Whistle is sick. Dixie just told me the news. He's in your bed.'

Jason was supposed to help his group clean down the BBQs after dinner. He leaned over to Brett sitting on his left.

'Brett,' he whispered in a faint voice. 'Mate, you're gonna have to cover for me. I have a problem. I'm supposed to clean these BBQs, but I need to be somewhere else.'

'What? What do you mean somewhere else? What else could you need to do? You're in the middle of nowhere.' Noting the pained expression on Jason's face, he continued in a half-whisper, 'Sure, sure absolutely, but you're gonna need to explain.'

Jason slipped off while Brett brought the other boys who had heard half of the exchange up to speed. They watched Jason walk off as Sally leaned in to find out what was going on.

He didn't think they would be far behind him. No doubt their curiosity would quickly get the better of them but he'd rather have his friends note his absence than a teacher. Entering the cabin, he reached for the light. Whistle slowly appeared, lying on his pillow and taking up the indent that had previously been there. He was a pale yellow-gold colour and his eyes were red.

'My goodness, Whistle, what on earth is wrong?'

Responding in a croaky voice. 'Came for a quick sleep, woke up pale, sore throat and sore head. Think maybe picked up something strange from my prehistoric brothers at the parks. Something Whistle not used too. Cannot teleport, either, not much strength or I would have gone to grandparents.'

'What can I do? Can we call one of the other dragons?' asked Jason.

'No,' said Whistle in a firm hoarse voice, 'make all sick. Must stay here with you.'

'Cool towels might help,' said Isabel from his finger, 'maybe some fresh water and some sleep. I've been looking for reptile issues online. They can have flu-like symptoms. Maybe some antibiotics might help, too. Through Dixie I've told one of the young Z-dragons, named Buzz, what to look for at a vet. He'll bring it here soon if Whistle can show him how to get here. He'll wait till he finds an empty surgery and look for what we are after. It's getting dark; most surgeries should be closing.'

'Dixie, how did she ...' his voice trailed off as he realised Whistle must have called on Sarah to get her attention and then Sarah had gone through Dixie to Isabel. Turning to Whistle, Jason noticed his eyes were closed.

'Done,' he croaked. 'Buzz leaves it outside in the pot plant with the flower when he's managed to locate. He knocks three times before going.'

Grabbing a towel off the end of the bed, Jason headed to the boy's toilets to wet it down and bring it back for Whistle. Luckily, he had a water bottle in his backpack from the day's activities. He decided to fill this too before heading back to the cabin. He was just about to turn on the tap when the others showed up behind him.

'Hey,' said Brett, 'what's going on?'

Pausing, Jason turned, confronted by Jamie, Brett, Brad and Sally all with worried, puzzled expressions on their faces. 'Oh boy,' he thought, 'here we go.'

Wishing he had given this eventuality more thought, he realised all he had to offer was the truth.

'Guys, I need a minute. Stay here and I'll come out and explain.'

Disappearing inside, he placed the cool towel on Whistle's forehead and held his head up so he could take a few sips of water. 'Good?' he asked.

'Yes, Whistle sleep, okay?'

'Okay, but I'll be just outside. Seems I have a little explaining to do.'

Whistle, half-shrugging, gave a weak smile. 'Sorry,' he said closing his eyes.

Outside, Jason was quiet for a minute. Where to start? He was an alien who had a sick dragon in his bed. How would they react?

'Wellll,' he began, drawing out the word. 'You seeee ... I have a problem with a sick friend who needs to rest in my bed for a while.'

'A friend?' asked Sally. 'Where did any friend come from? I didn't know you knew people in Alice.'

'Well, actually, I don't,' replied Jason. 'He followed me here and now he's ... well ... not well and needs me to look after him for a bit.'

'Well, that's not so bad, mate,' said Jamie. 'Gee, it sounded a bit more interesting than that when you disappeared. What's wrong with him?'

'He has the flu, I think,' said Jason.

'Oh, is that all,' said Brad. 'We all got that shot earlier this year.'

'Is there something we can do to help?' asked Sally. 'I might have some Panadol in my bag. I'll go get it.'

'Wait,' said Jason, grabbing her wrist and whirling her back to the group.

'There's a bit more,' said Jason. 'You see, Panadol probably won't help. We've got someone bringing him some medicine, something a little stronger and not really for ... um ... humans.' His voice went up three notches as he finished.

'Mate, what on earth are you talking about? Now you're not making any sense,' continued Jamie.

'That's just it,' said Jason,' the Earth bit. You see, this friend of mine isn't quite from Earth. Actually, neither of us is for that matter.'

His friends were staring at him incredulously, wide-eyed with a generous hint of 'have you gone completely crazy' in their look.

'Great. This is going really well,' Jason said mostly to himself. 'They think I am a nut.'

'Maybe you should ask them all to sit down for a minute,' said Isabel from his finger. 'Earthlings always have people sit down when they have important news to tell.'

'What the ...' Brett stammered as Jason motioned them to sit on the path. He was feeling a bit more confident now that it had occurred to him that Isabel may as well show herself too.

'You see,' continued Jason, 'it's a rather long story but, well, I'm not quite from here. I come from a planet called Micoron, light years from Earth. I'm friendly ... we're friendly,' he corrected quickly,' and we don't mean any harm. There are a few of us who live here. We watch over your planet and ensure you're not bothered by the ways of the universe until you're ready to become a part of it.'

He looked at his friends, waiting for them to react or comment. They were all staring at him with mouths half-open.

'We have been here for years and no-one from your planet, bar a small few, know who we are as we enjoy living amongst you and assimilate well. However, there is a bad race who are currently searching for a new planet so the Keepers sent dragons to watch over your planet to keep it safe and ... you see ...well, it's one of those dragons that has fallen ill and is sleeping in my bed.'

There; he'd said it. Not crazy at all. The words had poured out so quickly he'd be surprised if anyone even heard them all.

'Dragons, keeps, wha ...?' said Brett.

'You're trying to tell me you have a dragon in our cabin? Sure,' said Jamie jumping up and leaping up the steps to their cabin. Swinging the door open he poked his head inside and declared, 'There's no...um dragon'.

The rest of the gang looked at each other before jumping up and racing up the steps after Jamie. They pushed the door wide open so firmly that it slammed against the wall just as Whistle opened an eye.

'Hi,' he managed waving a half-raised clawed hand. He looked bleary-eyed and sheepish to boot.

Jason, coming up behind them, pushed them all inside, 'Someone's coming,' he said. His friends stopped just inside the door so he had to give them another hard shove so that he could close it.

'Guys, this is Whistle. Whistle this is Brad, Jamie, Brett and Sally,' said Jason, pointing to each of his friends in turn.

'Hi,' repeated Whistle. 'Do you mind if I close my eyes? Sorry, Whistle's not well.'

Sally, recovering her composure first, said, 'No, of course not. Sorry we disturbed you.'

Taking a couple of steps towards Whistle, she leaned in as if about to adjust his bedclothes. She stopped and looked at Jason who smiled and nodded so she continued and pulled the blankets to just under his chin.

'Tanks,' said Whistle with a silly grin.

Taking a few steps backwards, she plonked down on the bottom bunk of the bed opposite.

'I think you should keep talking,' said Sally as the others found places to sit in the small dark cabin. Jason sat on the end of his bed; after all, Whistle barely took up half of it.

Taking a deep breath, 'Where would you like me to start?'

'The part about how you're an Alien and why there is a small dragon in your bed,' said Brett.

'Wait ...' said Sally, 'that voice. There was a voice earlier. Whose voice was that?'

'Oh, that was Isabel.'

'Isabel,' they all chorused.

'Your imaginary friend,' said Brett.

'Well, she's not exactly imaginary,' said Jason. 'Isabel is a very sophisticated computer that has attained artificial super intelligence and is the best of her kind on my planet. She has advanced so far I think of her as a person.'

'Why, thank you, master,' said Isabel, speaking from his finger.

Again, everyone's jaw dropped. Four pairs of eyes staring incredulously at Jason's finger. Jason rolled his eyes – this was going to be a long night. And it was. They talked for hours with Whistle or Isabel occasionally shooshing them when they got a little too loud and excited. They drew the curtains, hoping no teachers would disturb them. Isabel did as much of the talking as Jason, filling them in on bits and pieces about their journey and what they had been doing here. It was very late when Sally crept off to her cabin. They were supposed to leave early the next day for Uluru. Everyone agreed that Sally's large sports bag would hide Whistle on the way to the Rock. She would have to get up early and drag it back to the boy's cabin, splitting her clothes between the boys' bags. Jason top and tailed with Whistle who was at the unlucky end given Jason's feet reached his pillow while Whistle's were nowhere near Jason's. However, Jason wasn't completely comfortable either. Whistle, being cold-blooded, woke Jason every time his leg accidentally brushed against his friend's.

They were all woken early the next morning.

'*Knock, knock, knock.*' Three loud bangs on the door.

Jason was first up. Opening the door slightly he peered through the crack so that whoever was knocking couldn't see in.

There was no-one there. 'Strange,' he murmured to himself closing the door.

'The pot plant,' whispered Isabel.

'What?' replied Jason.

'The antibiotics in the pot plant.'

'Of course.' Opening the door again, he walked down the path. In the first of the row of three potted plants he located a brown paper bag, looking around as he did so to make sure no-one was watching. Shivering suddenly, he realised how cold it was and raced back to the cabin.

'Who was it?' came Jamie's voice out of the darkness.

'Medicine for Whistle,' replied Isabel, thoroughly enjoying being able to participate in the conversation.

'I think we're all awake,' came what sounded like Brett's voice but, being dark, you could be fooled as Brett and Brad sounded so alike. 'Turn on the light then,' continued Brett or Brad.

Flicking on the overhead light, Jason was greeted by his blinking, rumpled-looking friends.

'Augh, that's harsh,' said Jamie, shielding his eyes against the glare.

The smallest wooden table you ever saw, and a solitary chair sat in one corner. Jason seated himself at the table with the bag. Reaching in, he pulled out a vial of clear liquid and some needles wrapped in plastic.

'Whoa, boy,' said Brad.

'What?' asked Whistle, appearing from under a blanket? His colour was still pale, but thankfully he didn't look any worse than yesterday.

'Needles,' replied Brad. 'Anyone know how to give a needle?' he asked looking around the room and hanging over the bunk to look down at Brett in the bed below him.

'I can talk one of you through it,' said Isabel.

'I'll do it,' said Jamie, jumping off the top bunk with a soft thud. 'My uncle has diabetes. I stayed with him one Christmas and my aunt showed me what to do as she was off to her sisters for the holidays – hence my invitation. Anyway, I think I remember the general idea.'

He took the small vial off Jason, looked at the label and then back up at Jason.

'There's nothing on here about dosages. How do I know how much to give him?'

'About 20 ml should do it.' It was, of course, Isabel who answered.

'How do you know?' asked Jamie. Taking the needle off Jason and placing the small vial on the table while he took the needle from its packaging.

'I Googled it,' replied Isabel as if it was the most normal thing in the world.

'Oh,' shrugged Jamie, as if her response made perfect sense.

But for Jason, since today had already started differently to any other day so far on this planet, he felt he needed to say something.

'Isabel can tap into most communications now. She and Whistle linked into a satellite some time ago. She has access to elevated security if she wants, I guess. But they're just using it to keep an eye out for the bad guys.'

'Ahuh!' replied Brad, not at all concerned that Jason had just said aliens had access to Earth's security satellites.

Withdrawing the needle from the vial, Jamie was already tapping out the air bubbles. 'So, Isabel, where does he want it?'

'Subcutaneous fat would be fine.'

'What?' came the puzzled reply from Jamie.

'His butt should do it,' said Jason remembering his science lessons.

'My wha ...' said Whistle, looking a little alarmed. 'What is that?'

Whistle, having been quiet up till now, was watching the scene through red hooded eyes.

'Whistle, we are going to have to put this needle in your bottom,' explained Jamie as he walked towards the small dragon holding up the needle. 'It's only a small gauge. Roll towards the wall. You shouldn't feel it,' he said with the calm voice of someone who gave the impression of knowing what they were talking about.

'Swab,' continued Jamie, holding out his hand. Jason passed one to Brad who unwrapped it, handing it to Jamie using the wrapper.

The other three boys stared in wide-eyed disbelief at Jamie and Whistle. Unusual to see Jamie looking so comfortable in this situation. It must have calmed Whistle as he turned on his side as instructed without any further questions. After administering the needle Jamie applied pressure to the area with a tissue that no-one had noticed he was carrying.

'All done,' he responded. 'Now what?' he asked.

'*Knock, knock, knock*'. A soft knocking this time, as the doorknob turned and Sally's head appeared around the door before the boys had time to get up.

'Morning,' she said cheerily. 'How's our patient?'

Whistle responded with a small smile as Sally pushed the door open and entered, dragging a large bag behind her.

The boys headed to the toilets to brush their teeth while Sally commandeered their bags, stuffing her clothes in wherever she could find room. Jason hadn't packed heaps, so his bag ended up with most of Sally's stuff. Once everyone was dressed, there was little they could do except wait.

'So, don't you miss your friends?' Sally asked out of the blue. 'It must be hard going to a new school in a new ... well, I guess ... world.'

'Actually, I've been so overwhelmed with everything happening on Earth, I haven't had much of a chance to miss my friends. If I'm lucky, I should get to go home over your Christmas time and then I'll get to catch up with everyone and get back to some good old Micoronian fun.'

'What would you consider fun back home, Jason?' asked Brett.

Jason thought for a minute. 'Well,' he started, 'it's actually not that much different to what you do here for fun. We play sports, hang out with our friends and visit each other for dinners. We don't have movies as such, more interactive games where we create our own storylines and backdrops and our cyber-selves are the actors, so, I guess we're a bit more involved in our movies.'

The group were intrigued, encouraging Jason to continue this train of thought.

'Well, we might meet up at an entertainment zone with friends. Then we all plug in by putting on helmets and sensor suits and we enter a pre-chosen world to act out a storyline. We could be skiing on the Red Isles or hiking through Draco. It can be more of an adventure than a movie if we want. Am I kind of making sense?'

'Sounds brilliant,' said Jamie.

'Yeah,' agreed Brad, 'so when do we get to come visit.'

'What … visit?' asked Jason. 'I don't know. I guess you could come with me sometime. I didn't really bring a big enough ship to get anyone home with me this round though.'

'What … a ship … what ship? Of course, you had to get here somehow. Can we see your ship?' All this tumbled out of Brett.

The others laughed at Brett's enthusiasm. Blushing, he eventually joined in.

Sally, looking at her watch, glanced at the sun creeping around the curtains. 'Looks like it's time to get up. What were the breakfast plans for this morning?'

'Breakfast packs on the bus,' replied Isabel. 'They wanted to get on the road early and the park supplies packs for visitors.'

'Great, so I guess we have to see if Whistle is going to fit in Sally's bag and then get down to the bus, hey?'

Getting Whistle into the bag wasn't nearly as hard as lifting him. For a little dragon he was heavy. Two of the boys tentatively grabbed a handle each hoping that the handles would hold. Boarding the bus, Sally distracted the teacher counting heads, so that she wouldn't notice the boys dragging the bag onto the bus instead of stowing it in the storage area under the bus like everyone else. Racing down the back of the bus, they spread out, taking up the two seats in front placing Whistle on the back seat in the corner. Everyone tried to 'act normal' suppressing their nervous need to laugh.

Nobody on the bus took any notice of their strange behaviour. After about half an hour they relaxed enough to pick up books and games to while away the time.

'*Hrumph-zZzz-shoo,*' Whistle grunted, letting out a rather loud snore.

The bus erupted into laughter. Heads turning to look at the group. All were too shocked to feign sleep. Sally, the quickest to respond, joined in the laughter, letting out a loud grunt snore trying to replicate Whistle's. This bought more laughs from the bus as Jason caught on and joined in the laughter as if they had been laughing about something together. Brett, finally recovering himself, leant over Whistle, nudging him and whispering for him to wake up. Whistle, woke up but, not realising he was in a bag, struggled so much he fell off the seat and onto the floor.

'Ow!' said the bag.

By then everyone had lost interest and started returning to their activities. Jamie helped Brett drag the bag back onto the seat while reminding Whistle that he was in a bag and had only fallen off the seat.

It was a three-hour drive to Uluru. The group didn't relax again. Brett nudging Whistle every so often to keep him awake. On his twentieth poke the bag seemed to deflate.

'Jason, Jason,' whispered Brett alarmed, kicking the back of Sally and Jason's seat. 'He's gone.'

Jason turned to look through the gap between the chairs.

'Thank goodness, he must be feeling better then,' said Jason.

'What?' responded Brett looking worried.

'Remember I told you last night how dragons travel. Whistle is obviously feeling well enough to teleport; either that or you annoyed him so much that he found the energy. Either way, good result. At least you won't have to worry about his snoring for a while. We can all relax for a bit.'

After what seemed like forever they were eventually turning off the highway onto the road that led to the Rock.

'I can see it,' one of the students cried out.

'Coming up on your left is Mount Conner,' came a teacher's voice over the intercom. 'We can stop for five minutes, but we have to be quick as we still need to get to our campsite and erect tents, plus we plan to see the Olgas before the day's out.'

Pulling in just before lunch to the campsite they unloaded the tents before hauling them off to their allocated areas to erect. Unsure if Whistle would return, the boys set their tent up as far away from the group as they could manage. Sally set hers up nearby. Originally planning to share a tent with Kai, she now had a tent to herself, which was lucky because that meant she wouldn't need to explain to someone outside the group why her bag was empty and all her belongings were in the boys' bags. Tents pitched, the boys plonked in front of them, relaxing on the grass before they were called in groups to get lunch. It was then that Whistle appeared, peering out from behind the tent flaps. His colour almost normal.

'Where've you been?' asked Jason.

'Here most of the time,' said Whistle. 'Someone kept poking me on the bus, so I decided to sleep on the roof, much warmer.'

Jamie smiled, apologising but reminding Whistle about his snoring episode. 'Sorry, good news, feel better,' said Whistle, smiling back. 'Still must stay away from the other dragons for a couple of days but much better. Need to hunt, hungry, will come back a bit later to say hello.' Disappearing before any of them could respond.

After lunch, everyone clambered back onto the bus. Firstly, they would visit the Olgas, and walk through the Valley of the Winds. A warm day but the students were so inspired by the area that no-one seemed to mind – exploring with enthusiasm. Big red rocks loomed up around them. A presence surrounding them that everyone felt.

After the Olgas it was time for the hero of central Australia: a visit to Uluru. No-one was to climb the rock. A couple of students, having seen pictures of people climbing it, had indicated they would have liked to as it used to be popular. The sheer enormity of the monolith had all the students staring, mouths open. Walking along the path around the rock, reading plaques explaining the Aboriginal artwork on the rock and its significance, as they went. They would meet the buses after a couple of hours of walking and head back to camp for dinner. After two hours, they had hardly circled the rock. It was enormous.

'An eight-hour fast walk.' Isabel had commented.

Many students complained, saying they would have liked to have completed the base walk but all expressed relief climbing back onto the airconditioned bus.

It was late afternoon by this time, and they drove the short distance to the viewing area to watch one of the wonders of Uluru – sunset over the monolith. Then they headed back to camp for a dinner of cold meats, salad and bread.

Chapter 12 – Certain Victory

His plan was set. Captain Trane rubbed his hands together. The blue was his weapon. No-one stood a chance. No world stood a chance. Dragons were magical, expelled fire, clawed opponents, appearing and disappearing at will. The blue was his to control. Master Ezann had been working to completely remove the dragon's memories. But worse, he had been replacing them with made-up ones. Trane thought the best way to control the dragon was to make him one of them. Have him think he was Inkaba. Their pet. Trane had Ezann implant fake memories: the blue working for them, previous battles he had helped win, days of feeding on Sarth, a cave in which he slept near Trane's quarters. They even went so far as to place images of him hatching from an egg in front of the fire in Trane's quarters.

The blue had not woken. It was nearing the time that he would be needed. Just days from their destination, a desert, miles from anywhere. His scouts had returned, confirming there was little life around the area and plenty of places to land unnoticed. Small communities scattered about, each had only a handful of people. No match for the tens of thousands aboard Trane's warships. He would land in the middle of an island and work his way out to the cities, destroying as he moved. Enslaving as he went. Once he had the one island, he would erect his shields and send for the rest of his people. Soldiers would work securing the remainder of the planet. The island itself was as big as their current home. They would live comfortably. This world was abundant with food, resources and plenty of workers for his camps. His people would thrive for hundreds upon hundreds of years. He would see out his days here. A hero among his kind – written into history and legend.

Master Olingy arrived, clearing his throat, a second time.

'How long has he been standing there?' wondered Trane, a small smile on his face as he thought about the Inkaba's future on this new planet. Weakness. He'd shown weakness to Olingy. No, wait, he hadn't, he'd only thought thoughts. Olingy couldn't read his mind like he could the others of his kind. Trane's mind was too well guarded. He turned.

'So, we near our destination.' It was a statement.

'Do we?' asked Olingy. 'I am not aware of our destination. Seems many do not know; I have asked.'

'Yes, that is true. I fear we have a leak in our ranks, Olingy, so I kept our destination secret.'

Olingy fought back the urge to swallow. Turning instead to look out Trane's giant window which showcased black inky space.

Trane continued, 'Our destination is Earth.'

***

The day broke, the sounds of birds chirping woke Jason. Sun slowly creeping through a rolled-up flap of the tent, the air was brisk. Pulling the blankets around him tighter, Jason looked around to see who else was up. His movements stirred Whistle. He had top and tailed with Jason again but Jason had insisted he wear a jumper. Whistle had decided to stay in the area as his dragon kin were scouting the coastline. He thought it best he scout the centre of Australia. Plus, he was still in no hurry to interact with his kin after being so unwell.

'Morning,' said Whistle. '*Brrr*, glad I wear jumper.'

'Morning, Whistle. Sleep well?'

'Yes tanks.'

'Mmmmm … morning,' said Brett, a shake in his voice.

Jamie and Brad hadn't spoken but Brad pulled the covers over his head while Jamie rubbed his eyes, squinting at everyone.

'I guess we should pack up and go see what needs doing,' continued Brett. 'What was it, three hours to Kings Canyon?'

'Something like that.'

'Well, I had better go,' said Whistle. 'Lots more area to cover.'

They set about their chores for the morning: some cooked, some cleaned, some buttered bread, all in teams until breakfast was made, eaten and packed away. Then it was time to jump back on board for yet another bus trip. They would arrive at Kings Canyon midmorning. How hot the day became would determine what adventures they had when they got there.

***

'It's time,' said Trane to Olingy. 'Summon the blue to me. I need him to go forth first and wait for us. He is our secret weapon.'

How would they know anything of dragons? he thought. *The way they can place protective barriers over their hides so nothing can harm them while expelling raging fires that can melt metal.* He smiled, not a friendly smile, a malevolent smile – the smile of one who had already claimed victory.

***

Arriving at the Canyon at midday, the teachers deemed it too hot for a rim walk. So, it was decided the best option would be some lunch and a swim in the campsite pool followed by an afternoon walk. Their planned route was about six kilometres and could take them up to three hours. They used a bit of their lunch preparation time to organise some of the evening meal in case everyone was tired after their excursion.

Whistle had chosen to spend the day scouting so Jason hadn't seen him since before breakfast. It was great to just have a bit of fun with his friends. Easier now he no longer needed to keep secrets. Having mentioned the speed at which his hair grew, his friends had noticed it did look longer and had helped cut it for him this morning. Given it was their first time cutting hair, it now stuck out in places. They had all laughed when Jason took off his cap to jump into the pool. Luckily, he wasn't concerned. He knew it would grow back in a couple of days.

Before long, it was time for their rim walk. Swapping swimmers and towels for sneakers, shorts and wide-brimmed hats, they were about to set off when Sally realised she didn't have her camera. The boys said they'd wait for her so the teachers told them to catch up quickly and set off with the remainder of the group. They were fifteen minutes behind the first group when they finally started out. Sally had gone back twice, once for her camera and again for the backpack she had forgotten when she collected the camera. They had the trail to themselves.

As they were nearing the top of the first steep hill, all completely out of breath, Whistle appeared.

'Did you feel that?' he asked.

Finding her breath through exhausted gasps, Sally answered first. 'Feel … what?'

'That change, the air, environment, something is different.'

'No … nothing,' replied Jason, puffing too. 'Anyone?' he looked around at the others. Having doubled their pace up the steep incline to try and catch up to the others, they were all hunched over, hands on knees, trying to get their breath. At least now, from this vantage point, they could see the rest of the group who would be able to see them too and know they were on their way.

'There,' said, Whistle pointing off into the distance. 'A blue flash, did you see it?'

'Wha—' Before Jason could answer Whistle disappeared.

Reappearing where he had seen the blue flash, originally in the distance. Appearing in front of a large blue dragon.

'Sian, Sian, what are you doing here?' asked Whistle, both surprised and happy to see his friend.

'Go away,' was the gruff response.

'What? It's me, Whistle. What a surprise. I did not expect you to be up and around so soon.'

'I said go away,' replied Sian, swiping his paw at Whistle, 'I'm waiting … the Inkaba come.' Finishing, he exhaled a small flame in the direction of the small dragon.

Whistle vanished in surprise, reappearing next to Jason and his friends.

Everyone was getting used to Whistle's appearing and disappearing now. They stopped walking and waited for Whistle to speak.

Whistle just stood there, saying nothing, his mouth hanging open, eyes wide.

'Whistle? Whistle, what's wrong?' asked Jason. Sally, crouching down beside Whistle, felt his forehead.

It still took Whistle a while to respond.

'Sian, he ... he's here. Over there,' he pointed.

'Really,' it was Jamie who replied craning his neck as if he could see.

'Yes, b-b-but ...' Whistle stammered then, taking a deep breath, hands shaking, he continued, 'something wrong. Sian attacked me and said the Inkaba come.' Then, looking directly at Jason, he said, 'Something bad about to happen.'

It was Isabel who spoke first. They had all discussed the Inkaba. They all knew what Whistle was referring to. The others were too stunned to speak.

'Whistle, more Z-dragons,' said Isabel. 'We need to get further away from here so we can talk. Quick everybody hold hands.' They grabbed each other's hands as four Z-dragons appeared; touching the group, all disappeared, reappearing a hundred or so metres from where they had been standing. It was only then that Isabel continued. 'Whistle, send dragons to Jason's father and the Elders to tell them the news. We need to speak to Sian again.'

Another twenty plus Z-dragons appeared all varying blues and greens, purples, oranges, browns and shades in between. They looked at Whistle expectantly.

'Dad, what up? ventured a small bronze dragon.

'Moote, go to Draco. Tell the Elders Sian is here – he says the Inkaba are coming. I know no more. Go quickly.' Next, he turned to a blue, 'Ziera, you need to go to Jason's father. Tell him same message. He can report to Council. Both of you stay in case they have messages for you to return, and you ...' pointing out another ten dragons individually, 'you need to go to Josh, you Migram, you two to the First Armun, you to Abun and you to Raindeer.' The last two were the names of other Micoronians settled on Earth.

'Now, what?' said Whistle, sitting on the ground to think.

'Isabel thought we should go see Sian again,' ventured Jason. 'Do you think we could get any more from him?'

'It's worth a try. You should stay,' said Whistle to Jamie, Brad, Brett and Sally. 'Jason, you come.'

Grabbing his arm, both disappeared, reappearing much further back from the mighty dragon, this time in the hope of avoiding being singed or scorched.

'Sian, Sian. It's Whistle and Jason, I mean Jazz from Micoron.'

'What do you want?' came a deep reply.

'To talk.' It was Isabel who spoke this time. 'You mentioned something to Whistle earlier about the Inkaba; what about the Inkaba?' she asked.

'They are coming. We are coming to live here. That is all I know,' he said and settled onto the ground, enjoying the hot sun. At the end of this last statement he opened one eye and stared at the duo.

Pushing her luck a little, Isabel continued, 'Ah, the Inkaba, do you know when they might be coming?'

'Soon. Maybe by nightfall, maybe by morning, not later,' replied the dragon.

Jason inhaled audibly. 'Ask him how he knows this?' he whispered.

'Why, they told me, boy,' replied the dragon. Young dragons had exceptional hearing. 'I will aid my master to claim this land. It will be his.' He closed his eyes – ending the conversation.

Jason and Whistle looked at each other.

Isabel spoke softly. 'They are coming, the dragon leaders. Trixie just told me Sarah has been in contact with them already. I have explained what happened just now.'

Silence for a minute before Isabel continued quietly, 'Zion comes too.'

Whistle grabbed Jason's hand, returning them to the group.

'How is he?' It was Brett.

'What's going on?' asked Sally.

'We are in trouble. Something is wrong with Sian. He seems to think he works for, or is one of, the Inkaba and, worse still, from what he says, the Inkaba are coming to claim Earth,' replied Jason.

They had no time to speak. Their prolonged absence had been noted by one of the teachers. Isabel could hear their names being called anxiously. They couldn't let on that anything was wrong. Any attempt to explain might lead to mild hysteria.

Whistle vanished, returning moments later.

'I have scouted. There is a rocky outcrop ahead of the group that you could come out off. Unfortunately, everything behind you is quite flat on the rim and you would take forever to catch up to the group with them watching. From the outcrop, you could check in and come back here with us, help solve this issue.'

'Yes. Let's do that then,' said Sally.

Linking hands, the dragon transported them forward to the rocks. Emerging, they answered to their names.

'Yes, yes we are over here,' said Sally.

'Sally dear, how ever did you all get in front of us?'

'Oh, you must have been admiring the view at one of the lookouts and missed us passing. Did we worry you? Sorry, I guess we were so intent on catching up we walked straight past you. Lucky you sang out'

'Well, that is a relief,' replied the teacher. 'Carry on everyone; we've still got some distance to cross.'

Once the class had disappeared around the rocky outcrop, they flopped onto some nearby rocks to talk.

'When will the dragon leaders get here, Isabel?' asked Brad, speaking up for the first time.

'Any moment actually, Brad. However, you all need to return to your school group before your behaviour arouses suspicion.'

'What? You can't be serious!' Jamie exclaimed, flinging his arms wide to emphasise his point.

'I hate to admit it, but she's right,' said Jason, folding his arms across his chest resignedly.

'Any news, Whistle?' asked Isabel.

'I just heard from Zion. I go to find suitable distance for the dragon leaders to land. I update you all when I know more.' Vanishing.

The others stood up to catch up to the group but maintaining some distance so that it wasn't too obvious to everyone else that the five of them were talking furiously amongst themselves, occasionally looking off to various horizons, hoping to catch a glimpse of something out of the ordinary.

Chapter 13 – The Arrival

It was night when Whistle finally appeared in the boys' tent.

'Awake?' whispered Whistle.

'Of course,' replied Brett.

'We all are,' came Sally's voice from across the darkness. She had crept over to the boys' tent to wait once everyone else had turned off their lights to sleep.

'Yeah, me too. What's happening?' asked Jason.

'We dragons wait, far from here but not too far.'

'Can we come with you?' asked Sally.

'Umm … yes, I am told you can. Wait.' More Z-dragons appeared. 'Hold hands.' Fumbling in the dark to find each other's hands. Reappearing next to what looked like large boulders or hills. There was a full moon tonight so even though it was dark they could still make out a fair bit.

The large rock closest to the group suddenly moved, a huge head swivelling round to observe the group, dark eyes swirling.

'Jazz, son of Faroon, good to meet you finally. I am Martare a dragon leader dedicated to healing.'

Jason nodded, 'Good to meet you, Martare. Thank you for coming.' Jason was, as always, conscious of being the son of Faroon and therefore manners were very important – especially when conversing with dragons.

Jason couldn't tell how many dragons there were. Looking around, he noticed his friends had retreated from the dragon leader and were huddling closer together a few metres behind him.

Smiling, it was Whistle who spoke. 'Not fear. These are the dragon leaders. They do not want to harm you. They protect you.'

'These are your friends, Jazz? Nice to meet you all.' The dragon leader inclining her head.

Jamie, Brett, Brad and Sally started to unfurl from one another. Brett bravely took a few steps towards the large dark shapes. Before he could speak, a mighty roar shook the ground. Looking up, all five were knocked off their feet by a gust of wind.

'You,' came the roar from another giant form landing not far from the group, the buffeting of his wings driving the group to the ground. 'You drove my master away. He is much angered by your presence.'

'Sian,' it was Zion who spoke. 'Brother, what nonsense do you speak?'

'Who are you?' roared Sian. 'I have no brother. But you, whoever you are, have ruined our plans.'

'It's no use,' said Zion to Martare. 'I can't get through to him. All I see is black, with red raging at the edges.'

Martare ventured, 'Sian, it is us, those of your clutch – the Inkaba have done something to your memories. You are not part of their army. You are of our clutch. This is your brother, Zion.'

Sian said nothing. Staring at the group and then at the dragons, ten to be exact, swivelling his head from side to side he took them all in.

'Saranah!' said Whistle. 'She has reached him before, maybe now.' Vanishing, reappearing moments later holding Saranah's hand. She didn't hesitate but ran to stand in front of Zion who was now face-to-face with Sian.

'Sian, Sian,' she called, as she reached out to him with her mind, her hand extending. Visibly recoiling, she withdrew her hand, taking a step back towards the protection of Zion. She took a moment. This time venturing a little more cautiously, 'Sian, how are you? What seems to be the matter? Can I help?' Her voice soft, persuasive.

Barely acknowledging her, Sian continued looking from side to side at each of his enemies.

Jason spoke, quietly, just loud enough for those quite close to hear. 'Master Olin. Sarah said she saw him when talking to Sian. Maybe he's with the Inkaba and can help. Whistle, you've got to find Olin.'

Jason grabbed Whistle's and Moote's hands, this time reappearing in a room with control desks everywhere and a massive window looking out onto Earth. Between them and the window stood several scowling Inkaba.

'You!' one of the Inkaba exclaimed. 'Get them!' he shouted.

'Which one?' Jason asked Whistle anxiously.

Whistle looked around. 'There,' he replied, waddling off and reaching for a black-robed man. Striking out with a blue double-ended sword an Inkaba warrior almost struck Whistle. Jason, jumping in front of the black-robed figure raised his arm as he faced the Inkaba warrior.

'Isabel. Kill.' A red, not blue, light shot out from his ring. The warrior fell to one side, dropping his weapon. In the moment of confusion, the Z-dragons touched Jason and the Pedite, all four of them disappearing, reappearing next to Martare and the group of Earthlings.

'Whistle, what's going on?' demanded Olin, taking in the scene in front of him.

'It's Sian. He needs your help, Master,' said Moote.

'Ahhhh. Of course, he does. Sian!' he shouted in a rather compelling voice. The large dragon, hearing his name, turned his head. Master Olin, closing his eyes, sought the young blue.

'*Olin?*' came the question from Sian, '*you know these dragons, these people?*' They were now sitting near a waterfall in Draco. Olin had manifested them there to hold their conversation.

'*As do you,*' replied Olin. '*Wait, let me see if I can help you to remember.*'

Olin walked towards a door that hadn't been there a moment before. As he opened it, snippets of memories came flooding back to Sian: the first of another dragon, blue-black in colour, small they were, hatching out of a rather large egg in the warm hatching grounds of Draco. Then more memories of a beautiful land with two moons and deep forests.

Sian opened his eyes, as did Olin.

'Zion,' Sian said quietly.

'Yes, brother,' came the reply.

'They are not far, brother. We must send our kind. Destroy their ships. They can't be allowed to return to Sarth or continue to this land,' Sian, still rather confused, implored his brother. 'They are ruthless, hateful.' His whirling eyes, and the small puffs of fire and smoke coming from his nose were the only signs of the anger he was trying to keep in check.

Sian shared the Inkaba location and Trane's black aura with the dragons. Then all but Martare, Sian and Zion left to remove the threat of the Inkaba for good.

Sally and her friends, who had been hiding behind one of Martare's rather large hind legs, came out then, looking rather bewildered at the turn of events.

'Well,' said Brett. 'That's that then. I'm rather tired now. Could someone drop me back to the tent?'

They all looked at him, suddenly breaking into laughter, releasing the obvious tension the afternoon had brought. Sarah had joined them. Resting her head against Jason's arm, she too smiled at Brett's joke as she let out a loud sigh.

'See,' she said, 'I told you, you would save him.'

'Save who?' asked Jason momentarily confused by her comment. 'Sian? I think Olin saved Sian, Sarah,' he continued looking down at her and smiling. It was only then that he noticed she was wearing her pyjamas. Whistle must have grabbed her straight out of her bed.

'Not Sian, silly. Olin.' Her voice trailed off. 'You saved Olin.'

Chapter 14 – Not 'The End'

They were all so busy talking excitedly to each other about the day's events that it wasn't until Whistle shouted a third time that they turned to him, noticing the concerned look on his face.

'What's wrong?' asked Jason.

Martare responded. Olin, who had been scratching his old friend behind one of the ridges at the side of her neck, stopped what he was doing, leaning back on the dragon's front leg to listen. She had been talking to him in a quiet voice about everything he had missed while travelling with the Inkaba. Now she addressed the group.

'It's the Inkaba,' she said. 'The others can't destroy the ships. Their magicians on board must be reinforcing the shields. They are going to get away,' she said, shaking her head as she finished.

Olin stood up and began pacing up and down, rubbing his fingers through his small beard.

Jason, the twins, Sally and Jamie just stared while Saranah closed her eyes to talk to the other dragons.

'We could ...' Jason's voice trailed off. 'No, that would never work.' Pacing, stopping, pacing again, finally turning to Olin. 'Olin, how many magicians are we talking about? Maybe the Z-dragons could board the ship and teleport them off.'

'No, no, that wouldn't work. The magicians are far too powerful. To teleport them, the dragons would need to touch the magician and a Z-dragon would not survive such an encounter.'

Olin resumed his pacing for a couple more loops. Then he turned to face the others, his index finger raised and a slight smile flickering on his lips.

'Good work though, Jazz. You have given me an idea – the self-destruct. Each of the Inkaba ships has a self-destruct code. Their weakness as a race is that they would rather die than ever surrender. We could teleport in and use the

code. There is a fifteen second countdown. We could be out of there before ...'
he didn't finish just shook his head.

'Great. What's the code? Whistle, Moote, let's go,' said Jason, reaching for
Whistle's claw.

'No, it's no good,' replied Olin. 'The code is in the ship's log. I am sure I
would no longer have access to that log.'

'How do you know?' said Jason. 'We have to try.'

'No, it's no good,' repeated Olin. 'Too great a risk for such a slim chance of
success.' He paused, then resumed his musings. 'Unlessss,' drawing out the
's' as he stroked his beard, 'there is a way, but you would have to assist me,
Jason, as there are two ships and we must deactivate the shields
simultaneously or the Inkaba might realise our plan.'

'Of course, Olin, I must help.'

'Paper then, I'll need paper and a pen.'

'In our tent,' cried Jamie, 'there is paper and a pencil on my bed. Whistle,
could you?'

Whistle, disappearing before Jamie had finished his request, reappeared
soon after, holding a notebook and a pencil. Taking the items, Olin leaned on
Martare's thick hide and sketched a quick layout of the Inkaba ship with
instructions for Jason to follow once Whistle beamed him in. Olin then explained
the map, the control pad and its symbols to Jason, who now understood why
he had to go. Whistle would never be able to manage the buttons and knobs
on the control panel with his claws, although Whistle exclaimed numerous times
it was far too dangerous for Jason and that he should be the one to go.

'No, Whistle, Jazz must go. You will protect him. If something goes wrong,
beam to your brothers outside; they will protect you both,' said Martare.

'Oh, Jason, this seems far too dangerous. Isn't there another way?' It was
Sally.

Noting Sally's concern for Jason, Brett piped up, 'She's right, Jason. This
doesn't sound safe, mate. Can't we just let them win this one. The dragons
have scared them away.'

Turning to his friends, Jason responded, 'Yes, they have left this planet for
now, but the dragons can't stay here forever to protect us. As soon as they

leave the Inkaba will come back or they'll find some other planet to invade. We must destroy them.' He finished with way more bravado than he felt. 'Olin, let's go.'

Olin and Jason reached for the claws of Whistle and Moote and all four vanished. Sally grabbed Brett's hand, squeezing it hard, staring at the spot Jason, Whistle, Olin and Moote had just vacated. The four friends then sat down with Martare, Sian and Zion to await their return. Sarah sat on Sian's front leg, her head resting on his hide.

***

Jason and Whistle appeared in the spot Olin had vacated. He had Moote appear momentarily where Whistle and Jason needed to land so they knew where to go. Whistle began cloaking Jason and himself the moment they appeared, which was lucky because they had arrived directly in front of a magician. However, her eyes were closed, her hands clenched around a large white egg-shaped rock attached to a long wooden staff. The rock showed traces of purple and red veins running through it. They didn't waste any time. Jason motioned to Whistle and the two of them backed towards the door. They had obviously arrived in the magician's quarters as there were old textbooks, empty wine glasses and a bed with rumpled sheets nearby. The magician was sitting at a small grey desk, on which her wrists rested clasping the white stone in both hands.

Once outside in the corridor, Jason pulled the map from his pocket, unfolding it quickly. Not brave enough to talk, Jason pointed to Whistle to move ahead. Whistle had uncloaked them now as any magician on board might notice their magic ripples, alerting others. Either way they were in danger of being discovered as they hurriedly made their way along the corridor with its dark grey walls and grated metal floor which made a slight noise as Whistle's tail brushed back and forth across the surface. Jason glared at Whistle, pointing with his nose at the offending tail. Whistle lifted it off the ground with a guilty grin and a shrug. Soon they came across a black door that Olin had circled on the map. Trying the handle only proved it was locked. Jason looked around for something that might assist but it was Whistle who reached out, a soft light slowly growing from his claw as the handle began to turn. They slipped through the open door just in time as they heard heavy footsteps approaching then passing as they softly closed the door.

'Click.'

They were in a small room with control panels covering every wall. Jason looked at his map again, breathing heavily now as he realised how close they had come to being caught. His hands were shaking. He could hear his heart pounding in his chest. He needed to find a panel with a long row of green buttons. Not knowing how to turn on the lights in the room, they were left with just the soft glow of the buttons on the control panels themselves.

'Great,' thought Jason, 'a needle in a haystack.' In front of him were thousands of buttons, glowing a myriad of reds, greens and yellows. Suddenly he realised something was very wrong. Where was Isabel? Looking down he noticed a large crack down the middle of his ring. No wonder Isabel had been quiet. Somehow his ring had been damaged. His heart sank.

'I can't see a thing,' whispered Jason. 'This is hopeless,' a huge weight settling on his shoulders, panic creeping in.

'Not hopeless,' said a deep voice from the control panel.

'Isabel?' inquired Jason, his spirits suddenly lifting.

'I am here, Jason.'

'But how?'

'Not now. The buttons you seek are here, in this panel … nine, no, ten rows from the top.'

'Iz, you're a star,' he said, his fingers trailing down the rows of buttons until he reached a set all glowing green. Taking a deep breath, he pushed them one at a time, pausing only long enough at the last one to grab Whistle's claw.

'That's it, lets—'

Whistle was way ahead of him. Disappearing and reappearing again in the room with the Wizard and the white egg-like rock. Without hesitating, Whistle grabbed the staff, ripping it from the wizard's hands. It was easy as she wasn't expecting anyone. 'Grab my shoulder.' Vanishing again this time reappearing in front of the group on Earth – Olin already there.

'You had us worried, Jason. What took you so long?' It was Brad reaching forward to grab his mate's hand.

'The room was full of buttons,' said Jason. 'Plus, there were really long corridors to get to it. Luckily Isabel found the green ones and showed them to us.'

'Three cheers for Isabel then,' said Brad.

'Well done, Isabel.' said Sally.

'Yes, excellent work,' agreed Olin.

Jason looked down at Isabel, a yellow cord was hanging from his ring which he pushed back in with his fingernail.

There was a pause before Dixie responded.

'She says thank you.'

'Yes, it seems Isabel has had an accident,' said Jason, holding up his finger for his friends to inspect.

'Izzy is fine,' said Dixie. 'She assures me it's just a speaker issue which also affected her transmitter to your ear but, if she could impose on Whistle, once he's rested of course, to whiz her home, they can easily pop her into a new ring and she'll be as good as new.'

'There,' said Martare raising her head and looking into the sky. The others followed her gaze to where two large dots of light got bigger and bigger and then vanished. 'It is done. My kin have confirmed the explosions. There were no survivors. Earth is safe.'

Jamie let out a loud cheer, closely followed by his friends. Whistle, caught up in the moment, let out a thundering bugle and was quickly chastised by Olin.

'Quietly now, Whistle, the kids are loud enough. You … you could wake an army,' Olin said this firmly but there was a hint of a smile at the corner of his lips and everyone else continued celebrating with much shaking of hands, hugs and many slaps on the back for Jason.

Zion, who had been quiet until now, turned to his brother. 'It is over, Sian. Come let's go home and work on making you better.'

'Yes, brother,' replied Sian and they both vanished.

Martare turned to Olin. 'Master Olin, would you like to return with me to Draco? I am sure the other Keepers can collect you from our planet much faster than from here and I yearn to return home now.'

'Yes, thank you, Martare, that would be a treat.' He turned to Jason, resting a hand on his shoulder. 'Good work, son. Your father will be most proud of you.'

'Wait.' It was Whistle. He was still carrying the staff with the large egg-shaped rock which he now held up to Martare. 'It called to me,' said Whistle. 'It asked if it could go home now; it's been a long time in this egg.'

Olin reaching out took the staff. He then turned, stepped up onto Martare's front leg and, grabbing a spine above his massive shoulder, they were gone.

'What was that?' Jason asked Whistle.

'Long ago, black robes stole eggs from our hatching ground. I believe some of the black robes have been using those eggs to aid their magic. It's time that egg was allowed to hatch or die.'

'Wow,' said Jamie, 'that was really cool. They were all so cool. Jason, is everyone on your planet so ... well ... interesting?'

Jason laughed. 'And more,' he said.

***

They found out later that Master Olin had finally managed to come up with a way to stop the attack on Sian's memories by gathering all the remnants of Sian's tattered thoughts and recollections and locking them away behind a large black door in the recesses of Sian's mind. None of the other Inkaba magicians had noted the door but, unfortunately, by hiding what remained of Sian's true consciousness, he had also allowed the magicians to take complete control of the dragon.

But, as with any dragon, the ability to share thoughts and memories remained. Over time, Sian would regain most of the missing pieces of his life with the aid of his brother and dragon kin. Plus, he was young and had so many more experiences to store.

Epilogue

It turned out that the female Micoronian spy had managed to achieve great things amongst the Inkaba that had remained on Sarth. When the Inkaba warriors failed to return, she convinced the remaining Inkaba that it was time for them to throw down their arms and live *with* the Sarthians. She implored them for the wellbeing of their families. Weren't they tired of losing loved ones? She then brokered a deal with the Council of Keepers and the Sarthians. The Inkaba would be allowed to remain on Sarth on the proviso that they would never again carry arms and that they would work with the Sarthians to return the planet to its former glory.

For far too long the Inkaba had lost their husbands and children to war and had never had a place to call home. They had destroyed their world many years before. The Sarthians, on the other hand, were a very forgiving race. It would take them time to trust the Inkaba but they knew their world would return to its previous level of productivity much more quickly with their assistance.

All the Inkaba seemed happy, except one – the son of a great leader, Captain Trane of the Inkaba. Once he had been heir to great power but now he had nothing. Nothing but weak, snivelling turncoats happy to pander to the will of their enemy. But not him. No. His brothers and sisters would revenge the death of their father. They would take back what was rightfully theirs.

***

It was Christmas and Jason was heading home to Micoron for the holidays. He could barely wait to see his old friends and stay in his own pod with his Micoronian technology and games – not to mention his family.

It was going to be an interesting visit, however, as his new Earth friends were coming too after his grandparents offered to chaperon them.

Of course, their families thought they were going camping for six weeks having waved them off as they drove away in Jason's grandfather's fully laden

4WD. Jason couldn't wait for them to see his home planet and meet his Micoronian friends. Little did he know what was coming and that, once again, his life would be placed in peril.

***

She sat on a large bolder by the edge a dark river, a cool breeze raising lumps on her skin. It was dusk. The sun setting over the trees and the sky was a mixture or musky reds and purples. The air smelt of the coming rain. Nearby, a medium-sized gold and red dragon lay basking on a large rock, soaking up the last of the warmth of the day as it came to an end. The corners of the dragon's mouth were rounded as if he was smiling – content in the moment. The young girl held a long-stemmed daisy-like flower that she dragged slowly back and forth along the water's edge creating ripples that slowly extended out to the other side of the river. Neither spoke, each enjoying their distractions. As the Sun finally disappeared behind the horizon, a small mauve dragon appeared. It extended a hand to the young girl and both vanished.

Saranah hadn't known the small dragon that collected her from the bolder she had been sitting on next to Elanth, the gold and red dragon. He had just appeared, reaching out his hand, and she had known she had to go with him. His pleas were in his eyes and in her head. If she had known then what she knew now would she have taken his hand? Probably.

She looked around at the interior of the cave she was held captive in. It was dark but the walls had a faint glimmer of gold. The small dragon thanked her for coming with him, apologising at the same time. She smiled and told him she understood. With that, he vanished and she hadn't seen him since. She hoped that he received whatever it was he had been promised. She understood somehow it was a matter of life and death for him.

Book Two: Finding Saranah

Chapter 1 – Away

'They're never going to let us go for six weeks,' announced Brett dramatically, falling onto the end of the couch in resignation.

Sally, Brett, Jamie and Jason lounged across bean bags and an L-shaped grey lounge in Jason's grandparents' home.

Located in Darwin in the Northern Territory, it was currently 38 degrees outside so Frieda flicked on the aircon in the lounge for the friends while she made calls.

Jamie shrugged, 'I'm sure it won't be a problem for me. Mum's always keen to ship me off for the holidays. Plus I'm sure she'd love some extra time alone with her new boyfriend, Bradly.'

'Auugghh, how did she start dating someone with my name,' complained Brad. 'It's weird every time you or your mum talks about him. It's just weird.'

Laughing, Sally said, 'Yes I can imagine. Well, I think my dad might actually say yes. We don't go camping and I don't have any siblings so I think the guilt will be enough to push him over the line.'

'Yeah, but it's Christmas,' Brett continued. 'There is absolutely no way Mum's going to let us be away for six weeks, especially over Christmas'

As he finished his sentence, Frieda walked into the lounge. Turning expectantly towards Frieda, the friends sat patiently waiting for her to speak.

'Well, boys, I have some good news and bad news for you.' She looked directly at the twins Brett and Brad as she spoke. 'The good news is you're allowed to come camping for six weeks.'

'What? You're serious, no way,' replied Brett incredulously.

'Wait, what's the bad news?' asked Brad.

'Well. To be frank, your mum was quite excited. She has wanted to pop across to England for years to see your Aunty Angel, however the flights alone for six was prohibitive, so—'

'Wait, Mum's going to go to England without us,' shouted Brett. 'No way. She wouldn't leave us behind. You're kidding, right?'

Frieda turned to Brett to confirm her conversation when Sally, always to the rescue, butted in.

'Brett, are you serious? Your mum has just agreed to let you go to Micoran, Jason's home planet. Galaxies away. Well, to be honest, she actually thinks you're camping and you will be, kind of, just not quite where she might expect. Just quietly, I'm pretty sure you'll get another chance to visit the UK.'

'Yeah, how often do you get to visit an alien planet?' Jamie finished. 'And, what did my mum say?'

'Sorry, Jamie ...' Frieda started to say.

'Oh no.' Sally's hand shot to her mouth.

'Your mum didn't answer, but I left a message,' said Frieda.

'Oh, oh that's good and what about my dad?' Sally asked, lowering her hand from her mouth.

'Well, that was an interesting conversation, Sally, and a tricky one to boot. I think your dad may have been keen to come with us, which would have meant we all would have actually had to go camping.'

'What?' It was Jason's turn to be surprised.

'It's okay, Son. Halfway through planning, he realised he couldn't go as the Principals Conference was being held while we'd be away. Lucky I was so shocked I didn't get a chance to say much to deter him.'

'Oh, phew,' said Jason. 'I mean, I love you guys but not more than going home to see my folks. I would have had to come up with some grand plan to cancel the camping and gosh, how would we even explain that to Brad and Brett's folks?'

'Yeah,' Brad added. 'Sounds like Mum's so keen she's probably already bought the tickets.'

Frieda's phone started blaring her favourite Dolly Parton track so she picked it up and wandered back towards the kitchen.

It wasn't long before she was back, smiling.

'Well, Jamie that's you approved to travel. You all better start making a packing list, keeping in mind what you take needs to look like suitable camping attire. Note that, while we can manage a solution to charge your devices, there won't be a lot of use for them where we are going. If you have a real camera maybe pack that. It will be more use to you.'

'Wahoo, are you serious? That's awesome,' exclaimed Jamie.

'Wow, who would have thought our parents would be so keen to get rid of us?' Brett said, his facial expressions ranging between happy and upset.

'Packing? What? Oh, no. What on earth should we pack, Jason?' asked Brad.

***